stages of sleep

Stories by
Nicholas Thurkettle

copyright 2015 by Nicholas Thurkettle

◇

This collection edited by Katherine Jurak

Cover Art by Kevin Necessary
Illustrations by Heather McMillen

◇

ISBN: 978-0-9966407-0-1

First Edition: August 2015

10 9 8 7 6 5 4 3 2 1

"Marvin Karl and the Whatsit He Found on Tuesday" originally appeared in *Front Porch Review*, Vol. 4, Issue April 2012

"How to Be Depressed in the Sunshine" originally appeared in *A Few Lines Magazine*, Vol. 1, Issue 4

"The Staring Man" originally appeared at *Subtle Fiction*

"The Culling of the Beige" originally appeared in *Blood Lotus Journal*, issue #18

"Tourist Trap" originally appeared in *Paradigm*, September 2010

"Homam, the Very Helpful Genie" originally appeared in *Silver Blade*, issue 20, November 2013

***

OTHER BOOKS BY
NICHOLAS THURKETTLE

Seeing by Moonlight (w/ MF Thomas)
A Sickness in Time (w/ MF Thomas) (coming autumn 2015)

◊◊*

TABLE OF CONTENTS

FOREWORD
By Dr. Kevin J. Wetmore, Jr.

Socrates: "Listen, then," I said, "to my dream, to see whether it comes through horn or through ivory."
– Plato, *Charmides*

Let us follow Socrates and speak of dreams and stories then, you and I.

In *The Odyssey*, Penelope dreams her husband Odysseus is about to return. She believes the dream is false, telling the Stranger that there are two "gates of shadowy dreams": the gate of ivory sends deceptive dreams that do not come true, but the dreams that enter the world through the gate of horn are true and come to pass. The irony, of course, is that she is telling this dream to Odysseus himself, returned in disguise. The dream came through horn, not ivory, as subsequent events reveal.

Homer's text, however, shows our ambivalence to the things we see in our sleep, our lack of trust in the stories our subconscious tells itself. Some are true, some are not. Some are true that we wish were not. Millennia later Sigmund Freud came to the same conclusion: namely, that we work out issues in our dreams that we are unable to face in our waking lives. Does not fiction serve the same purpose? Are not stories falsehoods that lead to truth and the working out of issues that we collectively might not want to face directly?

Do we not sometimes wake with a real sense of loss, or empowerment, or grandeur? I might dream of playing poker with Shakespeare, Dr. Zaius, and Mr. Spock while my fourth grade teacher stands behind me yelling "This way for hovercraft!" and wake up disoriented to the real world since the dream one seemed more "real" and "right" when I was in it. Does not fiction work the same way? We get lost in stories when reading and must transition out again when the real world intrudes, yet the feelings and thoughts provoked remain behind, long after the dream (or story) has dissipated.

Here are fifteen stories from Nicholas Thurkettle. What a wonderful, Tolkienesque name, no? A name to conjure with! And conjure he does in these pages. What worlds you will enter and people you will encounter! A wounded war vet who decides to hibernate and the supportive friend who watches over him. An old man who finds a place in his heart for a romantic gesture. A teen idol who gets a second chance in his twilight years. The existential, inspirational, thoughts of a waffle iron. A couple that finds their attempt at spontaneous romance and eroticism spoiled by their children. A morality tale about the emasculating dangers of khaki.

As varied as these stories are, if I had to zero in on a major theme in this anthology, and I had a doctorate in literature, it would be the loss of masculinity and the sense of male identity. The women in this collection are strong and self-assured. The men are not. They have a difficult time being vulnerable, yet they obviously are. I adore the metaphoric simplicity of "Evan after He Got Fired." Spoiler alert: after losing his job, when the woman in his life becomes the sole breadwinner, a young man begins to literally lose parts of himself. From Marvin Karl, who does not understand why the world is not like it was decades ago, to Swaygron Jep, who has no time for (and knows the percentages about) masculine heroics, Thurkettle's men are either totally lost or perfectly comfortable in very unmasculine roles. The narrator of "Torpor" neglects his woman to serve as the caregiver for his broken, sleeping male friend. Brandon and Haley's dad, despite his obvious reproductive success, must literally negotiate jumping his wife with all the spontaneity of the D-Day invasions.

But my Ph.D. is not in Literature. It is in Theatre. I knew Nick as an actor before I knew him as a writer, and there is a lot of the stage in this collection. Nick commits to every role cast in this book: his characters speak authentically, but retain the sense of play you'd expect from a man who has played almost every character in *Much Ado About Nothing* in a dozen different productions.[1] I laughed out loud at several of these stories. The author will play with characters, play with language, and play with your expectations. Nick does not just tell stories: he tells stories about people telling stories. He recognizes the importance of narrative and the stories we tell each other as meaning-making activities in our lives.

In the introduction, Nick refers to this collection as an album. I would go further and call it a concept album. Many (but not all) concept albums tell an entire narrative. While everyone in my generation recognizes "Another Brick in the Wall, Part 2" and its youth chorus of "we don't need no education," the song is actually part of a much larger arc telling the story of young Pink's childhood, the loss of his father in the second world war, his rise as a musician in spite of an oppressive society, his descent into madness, and his final decision to "tear down the wall." In the book you are holding, each story stands by itself, but then they form a larger arc that builds a picture of the world as Nick envisions it.

And that, friends, brings us full circle. As we sit outside the gates of horn and ivory waiting to fall asleep, we see the world one way, then another as we drift off, and then a third when we dream. All are just as real and just as true. Like Socrates and Penelope, Nicholas Thurkettle is about to tell you his dreams. Your role, as reader, is to decide whether those dreams have come through horn, ivory, or both. Good night, sleep well, and sweet dreams. Your morning will be the richer for having gone through the night with these stories.

❄❄❄

Dr. Kevin J. Wetmore, Jr. is the author of nine books including The Empire Triumphant: Race, Religion, and Rebellion in the Star Wars Films, Back from the Dead: Reading Remakes of George Romero's Zombie Films as Markers of their Times, *and* Post-9/11 Horror in American Cinema, *and the editor or co-editor of another dozen books. He has also published numerous short stories in such anthologies as* Enter at Your Own Risk: The End is the Beginning, Midian Unmade, Demon Rum and Other Spirits, Reconstructing the Monster, *and* Moondances. *An actor, director, and stage combat choreographer in addition to his writing work, he serves as Professor and Chair of Theatre Arts at Loyola Marymount University in Los Angeles.*

❋❋❋

[1]An exaggeration, but if you are ever in the same bar as him, buy him a beer* and ask him how many *Much Ados* he has done and which roles has he played. If he doesn't know the whole play by heart, I'll be shocked!

*Author's Note – The author does not drink beer. The author does appreciate a well-mixed Old-Fashioned, however.

INTRODUCTION

The prose piece I am proudest of, and which you can read in this collection, was conceived when I took a notepad to bed with me and determined to write down what came to mind as I passed out of wakefulness. I saw a TV show once about this cracker-brained inventor in China who brainstorms while holding his breath underwater, and even invented a special notepad to have with him down there. That strikes me as drastic, but I can understand the impulse. New paths seem to open up when we aren't fully conscious.

Naturally enough, one of the first words on my mind that night was "sleep." I wrote it down. I played with synonyms of it, and soon found my way to "hibernate." And as I pondered the nature of hibernation I found the seed of what became the story "Torpor."

So it was a successful scheme, and I got rewarded with a story. Most stories have a story of their making behind them, because writers are always shifting strategies for tricking words out of their brains. And here I am, at last, with enough words devoted to this form – the short story, the vignette, the flash fiction, the sub-novel, whatever you like – that I could smoosh them together and offer the smooshings to you in one package.

While many of the pieces here have been published elsewhere, and we can digitally publish at any length we want, if I was going to assemble this particular stuff under my name I wanted to pass a certain threshold where I could feel like I was really giving you something – not a snack, a meal, by gum. This collection contains about 56,000 words' worth of fiction. That's barely a short novel, although many of these old length categories are losing the practical meaning once assigned to them by publishing houses that had to challenge the literary necessity of every leaf of woodpulp. But by the vague and fuzzy inner calculation that leads us to most of our decisions in life, this length felt worthy. Substantial.

Another concept that the modern age has really whacked in the head with a board is that of the music album. The word "album" was already under serious abuse by the record labels with their formula of "one hit single + eleven whatevers" – a sickly thing to do to a word that can be applied to *Pet Sounds*. But now people can buy the song they want and slide all the songs around in the order they want, and overall the increase in freedom is a good thing.

I do love an album, though. A good album doesn't have to tell a story: the songs just seem to belong together. They come out of a moment or a mood. The songs on *Automatic for the People* stand alone as so many gems, but when you listen to them together, they say something bigger. That was the secret bonus extra challenge I set for myself: I didn't want to just give you enough stories to justify calling the product a collection. I wanted them to belong together.

But what the hell does a folksy anecdote about a grumpy old man who finds something by the side of the road have to do with a goof-off about centaurs invading our world? Or a language trance about a man all but floating through an unusual museum? Or a straight and serious story of a former soldier with an unusual plan to grapple with his post-war trauma?

I don't think I have a genre. I write whatever the hell idea gets words out any given day, whether it be screenplay, stage play, or prose. Certainly nothing here reflects the race-against-time conspiracy thrills of my first novel, *Seeing by Moonlight* (a collaboration with MF Thomas you should check out if you want some solid, no-frills reading entertainment). This lack of commonality between stories knocks out the natural tie-together for any kind of collection. If you like science fiction and fantasy, there are a couple of those pieces here. If you like funny yarns, there are some of those too. Some of the stories are very, very not funny.

But that word, "Sleep" – there's something there. I read before bed on many nights, and unless you're too flattened by your day to keep your eyes open, or unless there's sex to be had, you really ought to read before bed, too. To engage your imagination on the way to Dreamland is the ultimate runner's stretch – you get more out of it and it's good for you. How I feel each morning is determined not by how long I slept, but how much dreaming I did while I was there.

I should say that I am not a scientist, and therefore you should not trust the scientific veracity of a damn thing I say. However, when you read about sleep, you read about brain waves, and I did read once that our brain waves while dreaming are very similar to those when we are awake. I believe that – our senses are engaged, we perceive and experience and sometimes even think and act. What's changed is that the universe has turned inward and now operates under radically different rules. That's the dream world, and it is indispensable to life.

But what about what's in-between those states? That journey from our world to the dream world is its own hybrid beast. Some nights you won't make it to dreaming. Some nights you're robbed of a smooth trip back, and for a while you don't even know where the hell you are. Those make for interesting mornings.

I love this whole idea. It makes me want to understand the nature of that journey, and why it's healthy to keep these two worlds separated but eternally bridged. It makes me want to understand the bridge. You shouldn't just write about what you know, you should write about what you love. The words come easier that way. So as I looked at these stories through the lens of which ones fit in our waking world, which ones felt most dream-like, and which seemed to occupy some in-between place, the structure of a collection suddenly occurred with a great imitation of naturalness. And I loved it.

With a variety this wide, I am pretty sure there are stories in here you won't like, won't connect with, won't "get," or however you want to put it. Just between you and me: I am sorry, but it's okay by me. Some of the greatest albums ever made have a howler or two on them – why should this be any different?

I do really hope there is something here you will like. And I have worked very hard – by which I mean spent so very many hours learning, writing, rejecting, learning more, writing again, re-writing, seeking criticism from others, heaping criticism upon myself, editing, hiring someone else for yet more editing, reading about how to independently publish a book, and most, most importantly of all of these things, dreaming – to create the tiny possibility that there is something here you will love. Something you will want to tell your friends all about. Something that takes up residence in your mind, and becomes part of the churning stuff that makes your own dreams.

Wouldn't that be fantastic if that happened? Only one way to find out – this takes both of us, you know.

Good night.

❖❖❖

I. THE WAKING WORLD

"He felt that his whole life was some kind of dream and he sometimes wondered whose it was and whether they were enjoying it."
– Douglas Adams

"Life could be a dream, sweetheart
(Hello, hello again, sh-boom and hopin' we'll meet again...)"
– The Chords (James Keyes, Claude & Carl Feaster, Floyd F. McRae, and James Edwards)

MARVIN KARL AND THE WHATSIT HE FOUND ON TUESDAY

Marvin Karl woke up a half-hour earlier than he liked, because the damn Talmoon Creek Bridge was still out from that storm in April and he was going to need the extra time to get around it. He had written an acid letter to the Bugler back in May on the subject of important community bridges being washed over in April and still being unusable in May. It was June now, and he was indignant about that.

He read the paper over his coffee and messy eggs. That boob Stan who used to run the camera store had another one of his rambling columns. This one was about how the parking spaces at the market on Howard Avenue didn't seem wide enough for "these cars they make these days." In Stan's feebling mind, this somehow related to the Nobility of the Older Generation.

Marvin snorted as he ground more pepper into his eggs. Stan's ongoing refusal to find anything goddamn interesting to say was just rude. Marvin didn't know how the paper could invite the oaf to stand on the same weekly soapbox for going on sixteen years. Depending on what side of the bed he woke up on, he figured it had to do with either basic sloth or blackmail. Either way, it always made him grumpy on Tuesdays. He scratched at his mustache. Damnation on Stan for making his mustache itch.

Out his front door, Marvin clumped down the three porch steps, swinging his stiff leg in a wide half-circle. The weather looked okay. A few black bugs, more a scouting party than a swarm, circled his head while he crunched across the gravel drive and he muttered oaths of vengeance against their entire breed.

The truck didn't want to make up her mind about turning over, but Marvin kept the pedal down and the key wrenched sideways, and finally she gave in. The sun wasn't high enough to be out of his eyes when he headed east on Pipestone Road, so he squinted and flipped down the visor. He slowed down too, since this would be the time for some poor dumb critter to wander out of the trees, just when neither of them could see.

He made it to Talmoon Creek, and took the turn down the street that ran along it extra slow, just to let any higher powers, human or otherwise, understand the inconvenience to him. A month ago they had put up cones and poles and a fine big sign that said REPAIR IN PROGRESS, but Marvin had been driving past this point twice a day each Tuesday, Thursday, and Friday ever since, and he hadn't seen any repairs going on, and not that anyone cared but he didn't find the sign all that funny. He wondered what those crews did on weekends – take time off from not working?

There was something new was sitting at the bridge washout, though, next to the cones and the sign. Marvin stopped the truck and leaned his head out the window. It looked like a pole with a big ball on top, maybe basketball-sized. He got out of the truck, but left the engine running. Curious though he was, he didn't intend to hang around all day.

It was indeed a ball stuck on a pole, with the pole stuck through the lid of a big paint bucket. Marvin reasoned that the bucket had to be filled up with something to keep the contraption upright. But none of this helped, since it didn't explain why the damn thing existed at all.

He turned it around, and there the ball had a smiley face drawn on it; a smile with big cartoon teeth, big eyes painted brown, and some scribbly imitation of facial hair. Below the head there was a sign fixed to the pole with a screw and bolt. Black paint spelled out: TAKE ME WITH YOU!

There was a second sign below the first, this one with much smaller print. Squinting to see the words, he tried to tilt the sign up towards his face, but snapped it clean off its fasteners. He stomped up a dust cloud and cursed the son-of-a-you-know-what who'd made the pole and whatever third world ignorants had made the fasteners.

Once that passed he huffed back to the truck and grabbed his glasses off the dash. The former bottom half of the sign, now in his hand, read:

I am on my way to Christina Barlow to tell her that Sean Whitley loves her, and that until he can see her, maybe I can remind her of his stupid grin she's always teasing him about. After giving Christina Barlow's address, it concluded: If that's in your direction, I'd love to ride with you awhile, and you can sign my bucket and tell Christina when and where you picked me up and dropped me off.

Marvin knew the street well enough; it was only three miles away. Well, only three miles when there was a working Talmoon Creek Bridge. And then he realized what must have happened.

This hitchhiking dummy had made it this far, only the last folks driving him had no idea how else to get over the creek, and didn't care to spend the time to find out. And since whenever it had been dropped off – must have been since Friday, Marvin was sure he hadn't seen it Friday – not one neighbor had bothered to do anything with it. This was all typical of the human race in more ways than Marvin had time to number.

He looked at the rig for a minute. The hot air got thick in his lungs. He looked down at the half-sign in his hands.

And then he hoisted the pole in the bucket with the ball into the bed of his truck. It sent a lightning bolt of pain from his lower back up through his left shoulder blade.

✲✲✲

There was a long line at the post office, and only two employees. Marvin idly scanned the pictures of the FBI's Most Wanted hanging on the walls, and perused the line ahead of him just in case. That old hag with the giant perm looked like she was up to her usual trick of bringing in some oblong she wanted to mail to her grandson. She'd tie someone up for fifteen minutes trying to decide on a box and then act surprised that she couldn't haggle on the price.

With the other clerk hijacked, Marvin ended up with Norris helping him. Norris was generally polite, but he had passed fifty and still wore a ponytail, and Marvin found that offensive, particularly for a uniformed representative of the government.

"Six stamps."

"Do you want to buy a book? That way you can take them home with you, just send out your letters from there."

Marvin puffed out his mustache with his breath. He took the six stamps he'd ordered and held one up. "This is worth more than a coin and is about fifty times easier to lose. So do I want to keep these lying around my house until they fall behind the couch and I never get to use them? Bet you'd like that!"

With nothing to refute Marvin, Norris just gave a thin, silent smile.

This was the first conversation of Marvin's day and he didn't like how it was going. He lowered his head to apply the stamps to his letters, then summoned his patience and changed his tone.

"Listen, uh, have you been having any troubles, what with the bridge out?"

Norris thought it over. "Not me personally."

Marvin managed to resist his first, second, and third impulses, then spoke again. "I mean deliveries, stuff getting through. Are you finding people skipping the mail, trying to get things there other ways?"

Now Norris made a troubled face. "I guess if they don't put something in the mail, we never really know about it. Garth –he's the one does that part of town by the creek – says it took him a day or two to get used to the new route, but what we get's been going through like normal."

Marvin shoved his six stamped envelopes at Norris, then tried to nod his head in a grateful way before leaving.

✻✻✻

Every time Marvin looked in the rear view mirror, he saw the ball bobbing around back there with that maddening jolly grin. He didn't so much wish it would bounce out of the truck bed and thus his life, but he did have the urge to spin it around, because he felt that grin was saying something snotty, like shouldn't you be finishing your errands first? Marvin wanted to retort that he was the one doing this Sean Whitley a favor, and so he shouldn't be judged on the order in which he conducted his affairs. And these other stops were on the way besides.

He parked on the street in front of the hardware store. Next door was Stan's old camera store – still closed and vacant. Marvin smirked.

Inside the hardware store he headed straight for the fiberglass insulation and started piling up bales.

"Doing your attic up, Mr. Karl?"

That little simpleton Antonio who worked there hadn't even given him a minute to himself.

Marvin allowed Antonio to help him hoist some of the insulation. "Yeah, old stuff's been there twelve years now. Want to have at all cycled out before October."

Antonio patted one of the bales with pride, like he'd made the stuff himself. "Well, not to talk us out of a sale, but if you've already got fiberglass up there, it's guaranteed for fifteen years after you lay it. In practice, it's usually good for a lot longer."

Marvin huffed. "What the hell would you know? You haven't been laying anything for fifteen years."

The young man chuckled. "Whatever you say, Mr. Karl."

He insisted on continuing to talk with Marvin, about whether or not Marvin would be buying all his insulation now (he wouldn't), and whether Marvin would like help taking it out to his truck (he wouldn't, but somehow the kid wouldn't be deterred), and in all the dumb patter he made it all the way to pulling out his wallet before he remembered.

"Damn it, hold on a second."

And, squinting into his glasses, he walked over to where the store kept all shapes and sizes of little metal doodads. He scanned the bins, muttering to himself, then picked out a package of small hooks and brought them to the counter.

"You got a pair pliers sitting out back there?" To Antonio's apologetic headshake, Marvin rolled his eyes. "Some excuse for a handy store. If you weren't the only one in town, you'd starve."

"There's always the Home Depot over by the mall."

"You know what I mean!"

Outside, Marvin rummaged in his glove box and found his pliers. Antonio was already lifting the insulation into the back of the truck, following Marvin like some helpful ghost.

"What's this thing back here, Mr. Karl?"

Marvin had intended to repair the sign here; now he changed his mind rather than have to talk about it with the boy any longer than necessary. "Picked that up over by the bridge out. Some imbecile out west trying to get it to his sweetheart by letting strangers drive it for him. The girl's place is in town, but I broke part of it, so I'm fixing it up before I drop it off."

"Should you leave it back there like that? Open? Somebody might take it."

"Well then it turns into their problem, or that kid's problem for doing something so foolish to begin with. What do you want me to do, carry it around everywhere? Puh! They'd put me in straps!"

"Whatever you say, Mr. Karl."

✳◇✳

He didn't make it to the diner until 12:10, which gave him a metric by which to fully condemn Mr. Sean Whitley's interference with his day. He took his lunch at 11:30, and every waitress there knew it. While he parked he tried to predict what chipper joke they'd use to rub it in.

Halfway to the front door he stopped, turned, and looked back at the hitchhiker in his truck bed. He sighed as he accepted that his tardiness would not be the thing any waitress in there would pick to have a damn comment about today.

The little bell dinged over the door the way it always did, and the counter seat he preferred (so he could keep an eye on potential idiocy in the kitchen) was available despite the lunch crowd. But there wasn't even room for a potted plant near the counter, much less the pole in his hand. Irked, he took a booth.

The seat squished under him, and he pushed the thing against the window. He sat there, wondering just what kind of a goon he looked like sitting next to this thing with a fake face. He wondered how much worse it would look if it were sitting across from him.

Edith – big, saggy Edith – found his table, handed him a menu he didn't need and poured him water he wouldn't drink. "Who's your friend there, Marvin?"

"I want the tuna melt – if Luther's back there cooking he knows how I like it. And I'll do without the comedy cavalcade."

Edith grinned. "Oh, I haven't started being funny about that thing yet."

Marvin looked pointedly out the window. Edith wobbled away. Marvin yelled after her: "And a Coke!"

Finally blessed with a moment to himself, Marvin fished out the pliers and the hooks and set to work repairing the sign. Once he had it hanging by the new hooks, he bent them shut – it wasn't the sturdiest job, but if the thing had made it this far, it would survive the last few miles like this.

A mess of signatures covered the bucket. Dozens of people had carried this thing and admitted to it. Almost all of them ended with at least one exclamation point: *"Headed home from Disneyland – best of luck to you crazy lovebirds!...I wish I had a boyfriend like Sean Whitley!!!!...I.S.U. Tau Delts rule, homos!"*

When Edith clattered his plate onto the table, Marvin all but jumped out of his boots. "Cripes, Edith! First you're padding around here quiet as a cat, next thing you're banging every plate between here and the parking lot. Make up your mind why don't you!"

"Can't scare me off, Marvin; I still remember when you used to spank my ass and say we should run away together."

"I must have been drunk – three lunches a week with you is too much."

Edith waved a half-empty water pitcher towards him. "Now are you gonna tell me what that thing is or do I have to tickle it out of you?"

"You come near me and I'll spit in your ear."

But Edith just stood there like she didn't have a job to do, so Marvin told the story once again.

"You old softie!" Edith swatted his shoulder. "You're like Cupid, delivering a love note."

"I'm just old. I've got time on my hands. These fools went silly over each other long before they roped me in. It won't last, if you ask me; two people without half a person's common sense between them."

"Marvin, that's not fair; you don't know anything about the girl!"

"I sure do – I know she entertains a first-rate boob for a boyfriend!"

"It is awful shoddy looking."

And Marvin felt his mustache itch. "Now don't say that. I mean, he's a fool for not just sending a postcard, and I wouldn't trust him to build me a porch – but for just thrown together it did the job. I mean, he had to come up with something you'd see driving by, but would survive 2,000 miles with any clumsy jerk who might pick it up."

"Sounds like someone doesn't mind doing this favor half as much as he claims."

"Leave me to my sandwich, woman!"

❊❊❊

Ms. Christina Barlow lived in a snug place with a busted screen door nowhere special on a back road dotted with burr oaks. The only sounds were the bugs contending with the power lines. Marvin checked the address two, then three, times. Finally he quit the engine of the truck, and got out to fetch the whatsit.

She had five steps up to a narrow porch, and each one squeezed his stiff leg as he tried to maneuver with the pole; the ridiculous bucket kept getting in the way of his feet. He wasn't sure if the doorbell worked, so he rapped on the door frame six or seven times as well.

Seconds passed. Marvin looked back to the driveway – a car was there. It could be some girlfriends had shanghaied her away for shopping, or could be she was inside with her head clamped in some hair contraption that was cooking her brain along with her tresses.

But at last there was a shuffling noise, and the inner door opened. From what Marvin could tell through the screen the girl inside was young: grown, but not more than 23 or so. She was tall, with a long neck and plain brown hair straight down to the small of her back. Marvin couldn't call her pretty because he didn't like the plain-faced, gangly types, but he supposed someone else might see something in her.

She didn't say anything – she had a worried look that grew confused as she stared at the man on her porch. Marvin felt awkward and annoyed that she was leaving this silence in the air; it was discourteous. But he had better things to do than teach a kid manners, so he went ahead and talked.

"Look, uh...I found this thing out by where the bridge is out at Talmoon Creek. Said it wanted to be delivered to you on this sign here. Guess if you're Christina it's from your fella Sean."

Christina opened the screen door, which pushed Marvin back against the porch railing while she stepped out, staring at the pole with the smiling ball on top with its scribbled hair and goofy eyes.

"What...what is it?"

Marvin didn't understand why she was asking him, but he tried to keep his voice even. "I don't know what you call it. He just, uh, you know, he left it by the side of the road, like a hitchhiker, and had people heading this way bring it with them."

Redness spread out from Christina's cheeks to her neck as she read the sign Marvin had fastened back on, and she started sniffling: great, wet sniffles separated by little gulps of air. She blinked like crazy and her voice cracked out. "I don't understand; this is wrong, it's all wrong."

Marvin had not been expecting a reaction like this, and was beginning to wonder why he hadn't just left the thing on the porch and driven away. "What's wrong with it? You're Christina, aren't you?"

More sniffs, more gulps, and now little shining tears. "Mister, I...I broke it off with Sean two days ago."

Marvin felt like someone had just chiseled a hole into his skull, and that sentence was creeping in through that hole. "You what? What, Sunday? Why, for God's sake?"

She looked helplessly upwards. "I can't explain it. I just...I felt like I didn't matter to him, like he didn't do enough."

If Marvin had had room on that porch he would have stamped his feet. "Didn't do enough! Look at this thing! He made it for you. He'd already made it when you let him go." And a new, more horrible thought slammed unwanted through the same fresh hole in his head. "It was here in town! It probably would have got to you on Saturday if the bridge hadn't been out!"

Christina braced herself in the doorway and started shaking her head. Marvin had the notion he was supposed to give her a consoling pat or something, but the door was in the way and he still felt too sour regardless. He thought he'd stumbled upon an argument, though. "I mean it isn't my business, but I think he's, uh, proved his worth here. So you can call him up, you know, tell him it was a misunderstanding. It's clear he's sweet on you now, right?"

Like she was remembering he was there, she brought her eyes up to his, still shaking her head. "I can't, mister; don't you see? I mean, I know he loves me, but I already made up my mind to do it. I already did it."

Marvin felt his face go a hot he could not remember from any of his many years. He sputtered, clenched his fists, and got one syllable into half a dozen different holy condemnations of her and her whole family line before giving up on trying to express his rage.

The girl sobbed, retreated into the house, and let the screen door swing shut. "I can't, I can't deal with this right now, Mister.

I'm sorry...I'm sorry." And with that, she shut the main door, leaving Marvin alone out there with the whatsit.

Finally, he found his voice. "You're not even going to take it?" And just like that he seized it in his hands and dragged it down the steps with him, awkward bucket and all. "Well I'll take it. Maybe I'll toss it in that goddamned creek, too! You know you ought to patch it up with him – two as dumb as you deserve each other!"

Marvin hurled the whatsit onto a bed of insulation and roared out of sight.

✻✻✻

Marvin pulled back into his driveway while the afternoon was still refusing to give up its heat. He'd treated himself to a steak with his groceries and was looking forward to eating it rare. He thirsted mightily for a beer but wasn't about to leave the truck loaded. With each trip punctuated by his swinging gait up and down the three steps, he took in the bags of groceries, and put everything away where it belonged. One bale at a time, he toted in the insulation, setting it in a space he'd cleared near the attic ladder.

Tired, thirsty, and with his leg throbbing, he looked out his window at the last item still sitting in the truck: the hitchhiking pole. To think about it now, the right thing to do would have been to just leave it on her porch – make her deal with it whether she felt like it or not. He couldn't just set it out on the road again; some other helpful, unsuspecting soul would pick it up and walk right into that nightmare.

Marvin put the whatsit in his garage.

Later, after the sun was down, with the steak chewed up in his gut and three cheap beers softening the aches of a long life, he set his typewriter out on the kitchen table. He typed out the address of the editor of the Bugler, and with great relish began a new letter.

Our local government, if it can be called that, continues to have no idea just what inconvenience it is creating in the community by its failure to address the problem of the Talmoon Creek Bridge. One wonders just what they think their job is – to wave at park picnics?

The letter continued on for some time in that fashion. Marvin made plans to mail it on his next trip to the post office on Thursday.

❋❋❋

HOW TO BE DEPRESSED IN THE SUNSHINE

She lays herself before the sun, in a beach chair. Her wardrobe covers only her three most private areas – her pussy, her breasts, and her eyes. She bends one knee up, flexes her toes slowly, and tries to imagine her whole body relaxed enough to just trickle away into the sand. Her eyes are closed, and she is listening to a woman singing in French a long time ago. It is a hot, bright day.

She is wondering how this works.

✳✳✳

Megan woke in the grand bed she had bought after seeing it on television. It had all the luxurious comfort advertised, and she didn't want to leave it. She wished comfort was the reason, but it wasn't. She didn't know what the reason was.

I should buy a dog that will love me, she thought. *I should get an alarm clock that wakes me with soft, natural aromas.*

In the kitchen she squeezed fresh orange juice, letting her hands feel the skin and pulp and sweet stickiness. The juice was delicious, but she couldn't keep the taste in her thoughts. Every time she went for another sip, it was with the realization that some worry had replaced the memory of the last one. No continuity was allowed to her.

✹✹✹

Out on the beach, she thinks about her breaths – full and even. She imagines a cartoon cutaway of herself, with the air going deep into her lungs and out again, described by big, colorful arrows. Breathing brings peace. Peace helps you exist in the present. Existing in the present makes you happy. She has invested so much belief in this.

She tries to tune out everything but the sensations of now. She can hear the breeze. It should be enough to blow all the other thoughts from her head. She imagines the breeze as a generous, healing river, and she is sipping from it, one full and even breath at a time.

✹✹✹

Megan was in another meeting, feet out of her shoes and slipping back and forth across the carpet. She had chosen what she thought was a lively dress to wear to work – fresh white with black splashes; the saleswoman had been absolutely moved by the way it complemented her hips. Now she just felt conspicuous, and was simply hoping to get through the day with no one mentioning it.

Her team lead, running the meeting with his usual vigor, had a way of seizing unconsciously on a phrase for the day. Today's was *throwing someone under the bus.*

"The reason for these e-mail outlines is so that you don't get caught out saying something that can't be backed up. That's how you get yourself thrown under the bus," he warned, dancing like a boxer in front of a whiteboard. "Nobody on my team's going to get thrown under the bus; people upstairs want to do that, they're going to have to throw me under a bus to get to you to do it. So stick to these outlines, and the only people who will get thrown under the bus will be the ones who wrote the outlines."

Megan's fingers tingled with the desire to doodle a bus on her notepad. She thought it might be the only thing that would keep her from laughing at her team lead. But this would be rude: after all, he was only trying to protect her from a bus.

Instead she drew a little map of America. With it as a crude visual aid, she tried to pick a direction: she had vacation time built up. The world was flocking here for the summer, to enjoy that same beach she visited; and here she was, ungrateful, giving serious thought to flocking away. But where was the right place for her? Where was her good trip hiding – at some shopper's paradise? On a cruise ship? Among the million smiling faces of Salt Lake City?

Nothing seemed righter than anything else.

✳✳✳

She cannot remember the last time she ran, carefree, into the water. She comes to the beach alone and fears for her towel, her iPod; all things she knows she could afford to replace. She has not had to worry about money for a while, and she knows that she is blessed to be free of the worries that crush so many.

It feels disrespectful of her not to be happy. It feels disrespectful not to run into the water and splash in celebration of her blessings, to be young and secure in a free country that lets her wear a bikini.

Still, she cannot make up her mind to move from the beach chair. She feels she hasn't yet fulfilled the mission there, and to swim would be making an excuse for just another abandoned goal.

✳✳✳

Megan made sure to have lunch with Jonah once a month, because she wasn't sure how often he left the house otherwise. Years ago they had consumed six months by being in love with each other, but there was little potency left in the memories of lacing her fingers into his sweaty dark hair. In one horrible year he had seen both parents, a cousin, a grandmother, and a best friend die. He had once told Megan that they had been snuffed out like birthday candles. And so he lived in a large house with a pet lizard and insurance money.

She had made a promise to herself, which she had never shared, that no matter how far down he went in his moods and deeds, she would never condemn him, and never abandon him. She was going to hold this line in his life: to be the person who'd known him intimately, before, and still cared. He always accepted her lunch invitations, and she took this as an understanding.

"I was with a prostitute last night," he said over salad. She waited anxiously until he offered more. "So, okay, she said her name was Desire, and well, that was a lie of course, but she asked me to just call her Dez, like I was supposed to be on more familiar terms with the lie. Am I the only one who thinks that's fucked up and wrong?"

Megan made a concerned face and looked for a positive angle. "She could just be trying to make you feel more comfortable. I would guess the, well, the good ones would have all kinds of little ways of doing that."

Jonah slurped at some dressing. "Yeah, like I'm going to relax, when it's one-in-ten her pimp's going to break in and jack my TV, and two-in-ten she's going to turn out to be a cop."

"Has that ever happened to you?"

"Not yet; just a matter of time, though, really."

Megan remembered the night they'd spread a picnic blanket on the floor of her apartment, and eaten candy and played cards. He had worn a sleek black shirt that night, and throughout the night she had darted her hand in to undo the buttons – just one button at a time.

He continued. "There was this one girl; after we finished up, she said she'd clean my house if I gave her another hundred. She said she'd dress up in an outfit and clean my house."

"Have you not been cleaning up? It's a nice house; you should take care of it."

"I don't have time, I'm doing other things."

Megan moved to lighten the tone: "Actually, from what I hear, $100 is a pretty good deal for maid service. I mean, if she did a decent job of it."

The main course arrived, and Megan realized she'd been making her worried face for a long time. "It sounds like maybe you should meet women a different way. Maybe you could take a class or join a club, get to know someone there. There would be less of the...of the pimps and the burglaries that way, right?"

"Yeah," Jonah stabbed at his spaghetti. "But what the fuck do you know, right?" That was the only moment in the meal where he looked her in the eyes.

※※※

A man is talking to her, either because he doesn't notice the earbuds or doesn't care. She takes out the earbuds and looks in his direction. This time she hears the words but forgets them immediately. She sees the casual machismo of his posture, the tan and the physique and the smile, all of them fortunate. He can make her stir and feel shy, and he knows it.

She can see the play of the next couple of hours: she'll be folded into his group of friends, and there will be sports and flirting, but she won't get to know any of the others. They will be keeping their distance so he can operate.

She knows all the sensations, and can't say she wouldn't appreciate them along the way. But something in her doesn't want to be operated on today.

She can't stand that she apparently does more judging than anyone on this beach.

※※※

The car accident wasn't dramatic. Megan was backing out of a parking space at the grocery store, and slammed the brakes on seeing the car approach from the wrong side, but not before she felt her rear bumper touch its front bumper.

Her chest quaked, and an awful shiver traveled up her arms, and she felt guilty, so stupidly guilty. Had her thoughts been too far away? Had her gaze lingered too long on the little pint of ice cream sitting at the top of the grocery bag? The rumbling engine tugged her back into the real world.

The driver of the other car emerged. She had a few years on Megan. Her head was like a little pear nestled on top of a much larger one, and from the momentum she had in her yelling, it was almost as if she had started before their cars had even touched.

"...people driving every which way and putting my life in danger I'm just trying to pick up some dinner over here and I have to deal with this..."

That moment the woman breathed, and into that space Megan pleaded, "Are you okay?"

"okay well I guess you could say so you didn't kill me but your insurance is going to pay for this and I've got to go to the chiropractor my back's bad enough as is..."

Megan looked at the contact between their two cars. Nothing seemed damaged; they had just touched, like an Eskimo kiss.

Another breath. "I'm so sorry, I was the one not looking. I hate that it scared you, but thank goodness it looks like nothing bad happened."

The woman was silent, seemed stupefied for a moment. Megan re-iterated. "Really, I'm sorry. It's my fault."

The woman stuttered some, and tried to re-start. "Well, right...I mean, think about what could have happened. What if I had had a baby in there?"

"Do you have a baby?"

"No I don't, not that it's your business but imagine if there had been one in there you could have caused a real nightmare and you ought to be more careful..."

Megan felt her fist squeezing around her keys, and a tear swelling up to size at the corner of her eye. "Please, what do you want?"

Again the woman was stunned quiet. "I don't want anything; you ought to just take some responsibility. You can't cry your way out of it you know there's going to be a next time..."

Megan walked away from her car, away from the woman, into a coffee-shop. She sat by the window, even after she saw the woman drive away. Her lungs heaved.

****

She should invite a friend, she thinks. A girl from the office. Someone she hasn't seen in a while. It would be a good deed to be the one reaching out, a positive and proactive thing. It is the type of person she holds onto a vision of being: a person who takes action to let those in her life know they are special.

Everyone likes a day at the beach. Everyone.

****

Her date had found a route to her nipples and was sucking on them. She felt her muscles relaxing, sometimes sparking with little jolts of pleasure, and she stroked his head and hummed a little. He had made it a charming evening, and the wine and the low light and their conversation had done their job. It could carry on into a good night, she thought, and maybe this was what she needed – a simple pleasure she hadn't felt in a little while.

But as she craned her neck up around her apartment, she saw evidence of simple pleasures everywhere – her relaxation candles, and the photo of the massive, beautiful sunset that hung on the wall by her dining room table. She thought of the empty ice cream pint in the garbage bin, the grand bed – whose corner even now poked into vision through the crack in the bedroom door, as if asking discreetly if its services would be needed tonight – the three pairs of shoes which she had purchased but not yet worn. She lived among treats that, two hundred years ago, even kings would find hard to come by.

She sensed her libido shutting down, for which her date naturally felt responsibility. He squeezed her breasts in his hands, trying to re-start things.

Now it was all going to go badly.

***

She has been sunburned so often. Her skin is too light for this, her doctor has told her. And yet she has read that sunlight can affect a person's mood, that some people get such a glut of positive vibes from tanning that they become more addicted to it than caffeine. She wonders why this applies to some people but not to her.

She is worried that she would feel worse if she didn't do this. So when the sun is out on a weekend she is always there at the beach, in her bright bikini, calm and prostrate within the sacred revelry.

***

don't lie to us. They hold up their end by lying like hell to us, testing our limits every night, and bawling us out when we commit crimes like point out their lies, or feed them.

So one night Haley's at her ice-skating lessons and Brandon's "studying," which probably means galumphing around the woods with his friends stabbing lizards with sticks or whatever the fuck. It's funny that I feel like we'll ultimately be okay if he only performs acts of cruelty to insects and lower reptiles. If he ever gets to mammal it would be time to worry.

The phone rings and it's Haley; she wants to know if she can go out to pizza with her friends. Which means we have to get the names of all the friends that are there – it's like a game show for me and my wife, trying to remember if we've met their parents and if there's any chance they're that one we don't like because she smells like cigarettes.

But now we've got dinner to ourselves. This has been happening a little more since the kids got to sleepover age, and there was excitement the first couple of times that happened, but an awful pang shoved that out pretty quick. We had that masochist's loneliness of wishing our distracted, ungrateful kids could be there at the table, tapping at their phones and snarling at us.

Suddenly, though, I was tired of that. "Hey honey," I said to my wife after hanging up the phone. "Want to fuck on the table?"

My wife looked all over the table at the dinner setting, then out the kitchen window (to gauge sightlines, I'd guess,) then down at the table legs, then finally back to me, and after those many seconds she still couldn't speak. Then her eyes dropped as she looked within for the right sentence. She settled on, "Are you serious?"

I checked if I was, then nodded. "Yeah. I mean, we clean the food and stuff off first, of course."

"Of course..." she offered absently, looking again at the food. She re-filled her wine glass and took a large gulp. "You're sure the kids aren't coming back?"

"We've got two hours for sure."

More wine down the gullet. "Okay. Yes."

I was never so happy to help her clear the table. She scraped off dishes and handed them to me for the washer. "How are we going to do this?"

Maybe I'd lost my touch, but I didn't know quite how to immediately answer that. "I don't know. I thought I'd lay you back on there and we'd just figure it out."

"No. You have to bend me over it."

"I do?"

"I have to change."

I was grateful at this point for the dull, useful task of loading the dishwasher, because it kept me from wondering if my wife had been replaced by somebody else. It sounded pretty exciting – coming at her from that direction hadn't featured much in our lives for about the last ten years. I tried my best to encourage her. "What are you going to change into? You still have that pink silk thing?"

"No, God, I threw that out. The gray slacks."

"What, the work ones? I thought you said they were too tight."

"They are. I want you to yank them. Like, try to rip them."

"You don't have a lot of work pants." I don't chalk that up as being one of the smartest things I've ever said, but I was struggling to keep up.

Now she added a new twist. "And I don't want you to say anything."

"No words?" This didn't sound like an unmanageable deal. "Can I make sounds?"

"What kind of sounds?" I could hear a hot anticipation in her voice.

"I don't know what you'd call them. Like the 'uuhn...mmm' kind of sounds."

Now she turned her back to me, put her hands on the table, and leaned down over it. She turned her head and closed her eyes and I could see her imagine it. "That would be okay," she confirmed. "Just do it real low. Low sounds."

"Have I ever done it too high?"

"A little, sometimes."

"So you're going to put on the slacks, and I put you down on the table, and yank them, and I don't talk."

She was still lying there, picturing it on her eyelids "Yes. Only – come in from the living room."

"Okay."

"I'm going to be at the counter – ooh, I need tea. I'll be drinking tea." She stood up from the table and went for the kettle.

I tried for a compromise. "Well why don't we do it simple and straight-up once and then you can change and whatever else you need and I can get the tea going?"

My wife's normally the thoughtful type so I blame her reply on the strange flare in her eyes.. "You'll be ready again in time?" Boy, that question felt like I got stabbed by the Reaper's what-you-call-it. It must have showed, too, because she gave me a kiss and promised that my turn could be later in the night, and that I would be totally happy with my turn.

She asked me to turn off all the lights except the kitchen one. She wanted me to hide in the dark in the living room, watch for her to walk up to the kitchen counter and sip from her cup of tea, and then get myself in there, grab her, and give her the business.

I was a little nervous about the whole, well, non-permissiveness of the scenario. I'm not the pee-sitting-down type but I know the level of respect a woman ought to get. If marrying a good woman doesn't do that for you, having a daughter sure will. So I asked, "Uh...how rough do you want me to get, here? Are you going to scream or fight or something?"

She was getting agitated. "I don't know. Stop asking questions. Just get in there." And with that she scooted down the hall and left me by myself.

It got quiet and strange in that kitchen. I stood by the table and imagined railing my wife over it. Or was I not supposed to think of her as my wife? It sounded like she wanted me to act like some kind of prowler pervert. But was the prowler pervert supposed to give it to her good, or quick and sloppy? Was he supposed to care about her orgasm? Was he supposed to do weird things to her?

From where I was standing, I saw the calendar on the wall and realized we'd forgotten to flip it from March to April. I fixed it, and then I saw the reminder my wife had written in that next Friday was the weekend retreat my daughter was going to at her friend's church. First time I heard of the idea I got irritated that they'd probably spend the whole time trying to convert her.

My wife came back in; she had the gray slacks on but was in her bra. "What are you doing?" she asked.

"Fixing the calendar. You ready?"

"Do I look ready?" I didn't know how to answer that. "I'm figuring out what blouse to wear. But I have to put the tea kettle on."

"Microwave's faster," I offered.

"NO," she answered fiercely. "It has to be the tea kettle." I knew enough not to ask why.

She got in close and sniffed my neck. "Something's wrong," she said. I wondered if dinner was too much on my breath, or she could tell that I'd saved this shirt out of the laundry basket because it still had a good day in it, but I let her think it over. I have to admit, her standing that close in her bra was a lot less ordinary all of a sudden.

She made up her mind what was missing.

"You need to be sweatier."

I shrugged. "Shouldn't be a problem once we're rolling."

She grimaced. "It has to be from the start. Look, when you're in the dark, just jog in place or something. Get yourself sweaty."

"Only quiet?" I asked.

She took a deep breath that flared up her nostrils. "Will you please take this seriously?"

"I'm doing my best, honey. You're looking pretty hot right now, I gotta say."

She relaxed for a moment, and some of the strangeness in her eyes fell away and I recognized my wife looking at me. She gave me the tired and patient grin we'd shot at each other over about five thousand moments of marriage and parenting.

"Can I confess something?" she asked. I gave a nod and she gave a sheepish smile. "I really wasn't into doing it with you for a while."

At this point I didn't really know just how convoluted the path to this treasure was going to get, so I made up my mind to just roll with any surprise. This seemed so opposite the nature of the sweaty, lurking, pants-ripper she wanted me to be. Now definitely didn't seem like the moment to turn into that guy, though, so I answered her confession. "Like, when are we talking about here?"

"The first year we were together. Or so."

"The first year?" This was kind of stunning to me. We'd done it an awful lot back then, but hell, we were seventeen. That's what seventeen-year-olds do. "What was it. Was I bad at it?"

She rolled her lips in for a moment before answering. "Yeah. But I was too. Really."

"No you weren't!"

"I was good enough for what you wanted," she countered, with half a teasing grin. I guess all this was true.

I didn't know how to answer this history of disappointment. Wasn't like I could time-travel back and do her properly. I guess since she had gone ahead and married me that I must have at least compensated with other qualities. And we had gotten better.

"Bet you think I'm pretty weird right now," she put into the silence.

I stepped in and put my arms around her. "Nah – I just wish we'd tried this sooner. Think how quick we could rig all this up if I'd known."

She returned the embrace. "Good thinking." She stayed there for a minute, longer than I expected. Then she gave a great aggravated sigh, and tipped her head back to look into my eyes.

"You're going to hate me", she lamented. For about the twentieth time of the night I felt behind the plot. Seeing the question in my eyes, she gave another big sigh and tucked back into my arms. "Now I'm just feeling cuddly."

I guess it's time to stop skirting the detail that I'd had about three boners work up and settle back again since this whole scene began, and a body gets mighty excited each time that happens and mighty confused to feel it not going anywhere. No man stays a part of civilization without building a certain amount of willpower for getting over that and carrying on with his day, but these weren't your standard-cycle boners. These boners were for my wife, who is still looking fine, at a moment where we had the chance for better sex than we'd had in years. So these had been some enthusiastic boners. They were shanghaiing my brain with ideas.

I think what sealed it is that one of my hands dropped, and brushed across the fabric of those gray slacks. Because suddenly I pulled her away from me, to arms' length, and gave her a "No cuddling" so stern I even startled myself. And then I turned her around and gave her a push to bend her down over the table.

She yelped, but she didn't get up. Her palms were flat against the table on either side of her head. Her face was sideways, and the one eye I could see looked back at me with I don't know what. Was it shock through and through? Was there anticipation there?

I grabbed at her slacks and yanked. Nothing happened, although she made kind of an "ooph" sound, like it had tugged some wind out of her. I didn't feel so manly right then, not even to be able to properly rip a pair of slacks we'd bought at the Marshalls. I was more than half ready to give it up right then and apologize.

But her eye widened, and she whispered, "Again!"

I yanked them again. This time, I heard seams rip, and the tug took them about halfway down her hips. But the sons-of-bitches wouldn't just tear off. She didn't seem to mind though, she said "I've got it, I've got it," and she picked herself up just enough to unbutton them. Then she leaned back down onto the table and urged me to pull them down.

I wondered if she meant the panties too, but it didn't seem right to ask, so I just took them both down. She responded with a cry of "Yes!" that I barely recognized. And there were all her privates, exposed and available. Sure I'd seen them a couple thousand times. I'd seen a baby come out of them once (learned my lesson for the second time); but this time it was thrilling. I couldn't believe how much. Even as she started madly slapping at the table and saying "Do it! Hurry!" I was fumbling with my zipper.

And that's when the phone rang.

The phone is a horrible thing. It doesn't matter that six times out of ten it's a computer trying to sell you something, and two out of ten it's one of my wife's relatives wanting to gab away the dinner hour, and one of the other times it's the kids just calling to demand we let them do something, and that last one is usually nothing to remember at all. When the phone rings, the first thought that jumps your heart is that this is the Call. The Bad News Call. Daughter is sick. Son got into a fight. There's been an accident – oh Lord, how many times do you imagine the words, "There's been an accident." You can go years without the Bad News Call but you think about it every day.

You want to know what ruins the sex lives of parents? It's the telephone.

There I was, pants down to the ankles, ready to rail my sweet wife who was there on the tablecloth, and the phone is ringing. I don't know which of us swore first, or with which particular curse, but we sure ran through a lot of them in a short period. Because you just don't get to ignore it.

"Stay there," I insisted. "I got it." I went to answer it, only I had forgotten the part about my pants being around my ankles. So that was me face-down on the kitchen floor. I rolled over and sat up, not hurt but feeling like a fool about seven times over. My wife managed better at making it across the room and so she answered the phone, but I could hear that coiled up thing under her voice.

I watched her face change and I knew that look it changed into. It was a serious face. Something was well and truly up. I got to my feet and zipped up my pants and tried to get myself ready for the news. She hung up the phone, looked to me, and just shook her head.

"It's Blair's mom," she said. "Blair and Haley tried to take a bus somewhere and they got the wrong one and now they're lost."

"A bus? Where the hell to?"

"Well, Blair said to her mother that they were trying to go to some concert."

"A concert?" Suddenly, my brain rotated. "Wait, you think it's the band Haley's always talking about? Are they actually real?"

"Oh who even knows?" She looked at the phone, not over the news yet. "I'm going to call her."

I took the phone from her hands as gently as I knew. "Now come on, you know that ain't going to help. She's probably already scared to death to come home."

She answered, "Well, she should be," but in a way that I knew she was saying I was right.

I remember waiting to be yelled at when I was a kid, and at the time you can't think of any dread bigger than that, even though I never had to worry about my Dad taking a belt to me or anything like that. It's a different dread, though, when you're waiting to yell at your kids, and I understand now that it doesn't take up your whole world the way it does to be on the other end, but in a way it's worse because you've got all this confidence of being a grown-up that you spend your whole life building, and you know that you don't hate your kids, but you hate and fear to your bones the way they've smashed all that confidence in a second, and reminded you just how powerless you really are. You hope they're always going to help you do your job to keep them safe, and when they stop cooperating and start doing what seems like every cracked-up thing they can imagine to get themselves hurt, there's no preparing for how that makes you feel.

I looked up at the ceiling, and took a huge deep breath. "You want to go get her or should I?"

My wife shook her head. "Blair's mother is already on her way. Says she's about twenty minutes from them and that she'll bring Haley here. We have to ground her."

"Yeah."

"No, I mean it – you can't let her soften you up once we do this." This was one my wife had on me, I had to admit. I nodded in total agreement.

"We'll make it a week," I offered.

She grimaced. "I wanted to say a month. But you're right. A week feels like life at that age. And no Internet."

"Phew. Tough deal. Okay."

We had that sorted. And that's when I noticed something that seemed to need saying.

"Your uh, your pants are still down."

Still with only the bra on top, she looked down at her naked lower half and started chuckling. "My God. What were we about to do?"

Then I couldn't help but laugh either.

She wrapped her arms around herself. "I'm really cold now!"

And here the door was wide open, so I walked right on through. "You know what would be good for that?" She grinned and shook her head. "A cup of tea."

Now she laughed so hard she had to lean a hand against the wall. Her face flushed and she butted her forehead a few times with the heel of her hand, just to underline how ridiculous she felt. She answered, "Well, we do have at least twenty minutes, don't we?"

She looked up, and I looked back at her, and I think we both made a kind of funny-wicked smile at the same time, because she made a quick, clumsy shuffle back to the table and leaned over it again. "What do you say?" she asked over her shoulder.

I couldn't help but say, "You serious?" She nodded vigorously, obviously getting herself revved up again. So I put myself behind her and started to fumble with my pants, and damn it if my boner wasn't really sick and grouchy about wondering if he had good reason to come back this time. She slapped the table a couple of times, and I pleaded, "Just give me a minute!"

Then the phone rang again. From where I stood, behind my almost-naked wife, I could see the caller ID – our son Brandon. And goddamn, but that kid never calls with good news.

❊❖❊

TORPOR

I'm going to go ahead and say it was probably me who put the idea in his head. I still don't know if it was a good idea.

For the first two months after Darius came back he was pretty much full-time at his physical therapy, and then it took a while after that for the fuss at The Wet from seeing him again to die down. When we walked through the door, first time for him in almost two years; that was a legendary night. Josie and her two little girls spent all day stringing up crepe paper and tying balloons. You never saw her care so much about how clean the bar was. Then Darius comes in and tells her he missed the grime. Folks bought him so many beers he asked if he could start saving them in a bank, and we all laughed.

For about a month it was close to that level of craziness every time I took him out there. So many people wanted to shake his hand and welcome him home. It wore on him, I can tell. His smile isn't quite right; he's got scar tissue up most of the left of his head now, and that side of his mouth just kind of curls down. And while he'd laugh and drink and carry on mostly like before, the time would always come when he'd kind of look down and mumble, "Sorry. Just tired," and I'd have to get him home. He can't drive yet because, as he puts it, his eyes aren't working together.

A lot of times strangers would come up and thank him for his service. When I asked him how he feels about that, he just said, "I smile. It's what they want." I didn't ask him what it was like over there. I had an uncle who went when he was young. I know that you let them make up their mind if they're going to tell you about it.

But then people got used to seeing him around, and the boys at Swift Creek High were starting up football again, and that was plenty to keep the men at The Wet talking. The night I put the idea in his head was when, for the first time, Darius and I got a chance to just take our old corner table at The Wet and chew over our business in private.

He asked me about Kayla. He'd done that before, but I kind of knew he wanted to hear more this time. And I told him that she was still sweet, still skinny as all hell, and that her folks had been mad when she moved in with me without us being married yet, but I was hoping that come the holidays they'd warm back up.

"You're about one screw-up from her dad hunting you like a slow bear," Darius said. He always said that – like a slow bear. I laughed, because I hadn't heard him say it since he got back.

I wasn't thinking anything, but I felt like I had to say something back. So I told him something I'd heard on TV while he'd been away. "Did you know a grizzly bear can go seven months without taking a dump? 'Cause of the hibernation."

Darius didn't say anything for a second. His new face could look so still sometimes; stuck in that fucked-up droop. I listened to the TV noise and the rattle of billiard balls. And I suddenly got really scared, like maybe I'd said something wrong, and I started fidgeting with my chip bag.

But then Darius started to laugh. A real, bellowing laugh. I swear a tear even leaked out of his bad eye, catching light here and there while it rolled over his scars. He was gone, just taken over. His left arm was still weak but he brought his right hand up – that fist that's so big – and whacked the table with it – BOOM. His laugh went up high; he closed his eyes and brought his fist down again – BOOM.

Then he settled, opened his eyes, gave me a glistening look, and asked, "What do you think the first one sounds like after he wakes up?" And then he tilted his head back, opened his chops up at the ceiling, and roared just like a big grizzly might. Everyone in the bar stopped talking and turned. Even the people on TV shut up for a second.

I just about lost my mind laughing. I tried to do my own bear noise but I couldn't even start; just looking at Darius howling and thumping his fist made me laugh so hard my head started pounding. I waved at the bar to signal that it was okay, that Darius wasn't going to break anything. I know they were just trying to figure out what was so damn funny. How was I supposed to explain to them that it was about a bear alone in the woods taking the biggest backed-up dump of his life?

✳✳✳

About two weeks after that I picked him up from PT and we were driving home. It's about fifty miles, mostly highway. We had just passed the old burnt-down Graham place and the billboard where the trooper hides. I remember seeing a hit possum dead on the road shoulder, and that Darius had fallen real quiet.

He turned away to look out at the autumn trees and the power lines, and then murmured, "I think I'm gonna hibernate for the winter." His voice was smaller than I'd ever heard it.

I gave a little laugh; I wasn't following yet. I tossed my cigarette out the window and rolled it closed. I checked his expression, but all I could see was the hurt half of his face, the frozen one. Finally he looked in my direction, his eyes worried. "Like the bear we were talking about. Sleep through the cold. It gets too cold here, man."

I never remembered him minding the cold growing up, but he'd been in the desert so maybe he'd gotten more used to that. I couldn't come up with a question that didn't sound stupid, so I asked, "You want to just...sleep? Like, for months?"

The drone of the road under our tires got louder in the silence. Darius looked down at the floor for a minute, and mouthed a couple words so quiet it was like he was talking to his own chest. Then he looked up and ahead down the road, and continued. "Guess I wouldn't be able to sleep the whole time. I'd have to eat, go to the shitter: that stuff. But I think I want to, to just be in my house. Turn everything off, cover up the windows, make it dark. Make it a cave. And, just, sleep, as much as I can, until...I don't know. March, maybe."

Darius and I go all the way back, and I'd never known him to tiptoe around something. Even right there as I was listening, I didn't think he was hesitating because he wasn't sure he was going to do it. I was sure he was going to do it. He just didn't know exactly what was going to happen.

I was worried. I'd seen a lot of people in the last couple of years, people with job troubles or some sickness in the family, who would just get pinned down onto their couches and you couldn't get them up again for anything. My buddy Terence, I'd go over to see if he wanted to come catch a fish, and he would just say he was watching TV. Any hour I went over, watching TV. Smoking cigarettes. I'd ask him to fill me in on the show he was watching, just to get him talking, and he would just kind of go "Uhh…" and shrug. He didn't remember any of them, even while they were right in front of him.

But I'd never heard of anyone trying to literally hibernate. So I just asked, "Is this… like… depression?" It sounded stupid coming out like that. My hand flinched towards the radio knob to try and stop the whole conversation right there.

Darius pulled out his cigarettes and put one in his good hand. Then he lit it, rolled down the window, and talked between drags. "I don't know, man. I just want to sleep. I don't feel depressed. This is going to take a lot of work to set up, you know? Putting food away and all. I don't think depressed people do stuff that takes a lot of work."

"But you're going to come out, right? When it warms up?"

I saw a little of his new smile, and Darius turned to me. "Of course, man. If a fuckin' mine couldn't get me, what's going to happen in my house?"

Things could happen in his house. I knew that. So did he. He didn't talk for a little while. Then: "I could use some help. You think you could help me?"

I squeezed the steering wheel. I remembered the time my dad took me hunting and I winged a rabbit without killing it. And Dad was going to finish it off, but then he squatted down and took me by the hand and said, "You don't have to do it, but you should. Will you do it?"

There was no way I couldn't say yes to Darius.

❊❊❊

Kayla and I had him over for dinner. She set places and cooked up a real hearty meal, made an occasion out of it. It's funny that the three of us used to divvy up candy in the woods, back when I didn't even really think of her as a girl.

She chattered a lot; told him this story she'd seen on the news, about how they were making new arms that could wire right into your brain, so you feel things again. Darius still had his old arm and could mostly feel with it, so I don't really know why she wanted to bring it up. Nerves, I guess.

He's got table manners now. I remember putting down chow with him before he went in, and the mess was legendary. Darius loved to eat. I guess he still likes it, but I saw him cutting up everything neat, keeping his lips clean with the napkin, and standing with his plate to offer to help with the dishes as soon as he'd had his last bite.

"Hell, Darius, you're making me look bad!" I teased him, but Kayla just swelled with pride: he'd made her feel like a real hostess. She said we ought to do this every week from now on, and that she'd invite more of our friends, and my head ached just thinking about it. Moving her in had been a great way to spend more time in the hay with her, but a little lick of anger sometimes jumped up when she talked about making plans. It was like a lighter's spark: there and gone, and it didn't catch anything to burn. I didn't understand it, but it was there all the same.

Darius didn't accept or decline her invitation. He just said, "That sounds nice," and gave the smile he uses when people want to shake his hand. That smile they want.

After he left, I was having a cigarette on the couch, and she was still puttering everywhere, just moving things around the kitchen, stacking them and moving the stacks and knocking dust off things and making little sounds to herself. I swear it didn't look like anything was actually changing, it was just this funny merry-go-round. And then she asked if maybe we could go down to the Sears and look at a nice dining room table. "They do them on credit if we can't afford the whole thing at once."

That spark flicked in me. "We don't have a dining room!" I knew I'd said it kind of loud, so I followed with a quick, "Sorry."

Still, she spoke softly when she came in from the kitchen. "This is the dining room here."

"No, it's the living room".

"But it can be the dining room too, don't you think there's room here? For a nice little table for when we've got guests?"

Then I just blurted out,"Ain't going to need it. Darius is going to hibernate for winter."

Kayla laughed nervously, like I had when Darius had first told me about his plan, and for some reason that just made me more snappish. "What are you laughing for? You've never heard of hibernation? It's natural. Bears do it."

"You're foolin'," she said, only her voice dropped down low and that's how I knew she was worried. "You're foolin' with me. Darius isn't a bear."

"Doesn't matter. He told me. His mind's made up. He's going to sleep through the winter."

"And Christmas and all?" I saw her eyes drift over to a spot on the floor that I knew she'd been cleaning to put a tree into.

"Christmas is part of winter, ain't it?"

Kayla moved over to sit down by me and started to squeeze her hands, worrying one, then the other, like she trying to wring water out of them. "But that sounds like the most horrible thing.

Why would he do that? It can't be right. He can't be right. He should see somebody."

My eyes flicked to the remote on the table, and I remembered how my Dad used to put his foot down on a discussion by picking it up and turning on a show. I wanted to awfully bad, but I still thought I could maybe make her get it. "He does see somebody. Three times a week he goes to see people. Hell, I drive him."

"And is he going to stop seeing them too?" This got me, I'll confess. Darius did need to get his arm right and his eyes right, and the doctors were important for that. Shelton Haney down at the plant told him he could come in for a job as soon as he felt well. And the sooner he got back to working, the better.

"I don't know – he must have it worked out somehow. You know him."

But Kayla could tell she'd made it through to me, because she turned real urgent. "You can't let him do it. You've got to talk him out of it. It's a horrible thing. Nobody who's well wants to do that. He needs help."

"How am I supposed to stop him? Stand outside his place and bang on a pot? When he gets set on doing something, you don't talk him out of it."

Kayla squirmed in the sofa and made this sad hum from the back of her throat. "You could call the Army. Tell them. Promise me you'll call them. You have to promise me."

Then the spark caught and I was hot-angry. "Don't ask me to do something that's only going to make it worse!" I sprang up from the sofa and kicked open the porch door to go outside.

She didn't follow me out. I huffed a couple gulps of air, felt at my pocket for cigarettes that weren't there, and then just watched my breath make steam through the yellow porch light.

✳✳✳

"Beans," said Darius. "Baked beans. Biggest cans they make." We were each pushing a big grocery cart, and since the aisles were too narrow for the two of us, sometimes he'd just jerk his head towards an aisle and tell me what he needed from it.

"You want pork and beans?" I asked.

"Nah, I hate those canned weenies." Suddenly he chuckled. "First time in BCT I put a helmet on, Drill Sergeant says to me, 'Well I'll be damned, a wiener in a hat. Almost as big as mine.'"

We were the only customers in the store, so I felt okay keeping the conversation up through the shelves. "Was it like in the movies – guys shouting in your face, beating you up, climbing walls, that stuff?"

His voice got reluctant. "Kind of. Worse in some ways. Better in others. When they show that stuff they usually miss the point. It ain't about the shouting. It's about modes."

"Modes?" I piled ten massive cans of baked beans into my cart.

"Yeah. It's like, when you're at work, you're in a mode. Talk a certain way, move a certain way. When you're out at The Wet, different mode: whole different attitude. When you make love to your lady, different mode."

This all made sense to me. I sure didn't use my lovemaking tone of voice at work. Kind of funny even to think about it. "Okay. Modes."

"Yeah. Only when you're in, you need different modes to survive. You need waiting for duty mode. Out on patrol mode. Some dude's trying to break my fucking neck mode. Got to have all those modes at the ready any time, even when you sleep.

Takes up space in your head. That's Basic, man. Wipes out your old modes, puts new ones in place."

I met him at the other end of the aisle. He was picking out peanuts and dried fruit. "Hey, man, squirrels keep nuts for winter. Not grizzlies."

Darius stood square in front of me and puffed out his chest. "Maybe I'm part squirrel. What do you think?" He gave me this hard, killer stare and then, just like that, wiggled his nose. I just about fell over laughing.

The cashier whistled when he saw us coming. "Only guy I've ever seen with that many cans is Vaughn. You know him, says he's building a compound?"

Darius pulled out a thick roll of cash. "Yeah, Vaughn was our science teacher. Fourth grade, isn't that right?" I nodded agreement. "He was crazy then too. Told us that Major League Baseball was all rigged and that Ms. Adkins who taught English was a communist."

The cashier rung us up. "That what you're doing? You building a compound?"

"Nah, man. I'm just storing nuts for winter. You know the story."

"Sure do."

✳❉✳

A couple nights later I was laying in the dark with Kayla. We'd just finished and she'd cuddled up and put her arm on me, and I knew, just from where she put her hand, the way she held it there, and the way she was so completely quiet, that she was worrying about something. I asked her what was up, whispering it. *Bedroom mode*, I couldn't help thinking. Darius sure got that one right.

"I'm sorry I said you should promise me to call the Army," she said. "Can I ask you something else, though?" She felt me tighten up and her hand stroked my chest, kind of soothing. "Tell me you know it's dangerous?"

Soft as her hand was, all my breath just pushed out of me in one long exhale, like she had pressed it out. "Yeah, I know. But I just don't see it going bad. He isn't like that."

"You don't know, though. He's been away, and...things have happened to him."

I got more agitated. "I know things have happened."

She never moved that soft hand, she just nuzzled closer to my ear. "I want you to make me a different promise, then." I didn't say anything. "I want you to promise me, if you feel like something's going wrong, you'll break in there and get him. Will you promise that?"

"How would I know?"

"Just promise me."

Kayla and I had met when we were five. When we were thirteen we'd done some fooling around and then went our separate ways for a while. Even when we started going more for real, it wasn't like I'd taken her on dinner dates. I hadn't ever asked myself was this girl pretty, or smart, or funny, or whatever else. It's not that she was or she wasn't, it just didn't seem to factor in. One thing just kind of followed another around her, and it felt right when it did. I could get sick or fearful about what was happening, or even just angry or stupid day-to-day like anybody, but it was like a thing that just blew away and where I lived was somewhere underneath that all which was okay, and right.

Since she'd moved in I'd seen a couple of moments sail by where I fought an urge to be hard with her. It felt like what a man ought to do, but I kept not doing it. I didn't talk much about our home life with my buddies, because I knew they would tell me that a man ought to take charge as well as how to do it if I had to, and that I wouldn't be following that advice. I couldn't explain why.

I put my arms around her – she was wearing only a little T-shirt and socks, which she kept on because we kept the heater down to save money. I kissed the top of her head and sighed. "Yeah, damn it, okay. I promise."

I rolled over to put my back to her after that, which I guess was me trying to make some kind of point, but she snuggled up against me, and I could feel her taking warmth from my back. And I couldn't help but like that too.

❈❈❈

I got a look around Darius's place when I went over to pick up some checks and things. I was going to pay his bills, mail out cards, other stuff that would need doing. It was pretty empty. He'd given his TV and his computer away. "None of that shit, man," he grumbled. "If I've got to do something awake, I'm going to read." He'd put cardboard over all the windows. He had flashlights, dozens of them, scattered around every room. Flashlights and the fireplace. He said he'd use that for warmth and cooking. "So pay that gas bill, man, or I'm fucked."

"Your mom know about this yet?" Darius's mom was kind of a wild card. I didn't want to step on a tough subject, but if my job was to keep people out then I had to know what to expect.

"I didn't tell her. Went to see her when I got back but she's not too well right now." That's what he said when she was hitting it too hard. After his dad passed he'd mostly grown up with his great-uncle, but he'd died about eight years ago. "She might come around, though. Be nice to her man, she's my mama. But she doesn't get to come in."

Then he pointed at the table near where I stood. "Take the lamps with you. They'll look good at your place. But don't get attached or anything. I want 'em back."

At the door I realized something. "You're going to lock this behind me, aren't you? You're starting this right now."

For just one second it felt like my feet had been nailed to the ground. How was I going to turn around and walk away? It was an easy thing to make a promise to a friend like Darius, but when the time came? You ever have that moment where you say you're going to buy someone a drink, and ordering it for them feels good, and drinking it with them feels good, but when the bill comes you suddenly don't know if you've got the money to cover it? That's it right there. That's what I felt. I didn't know if I could do it, but the bill had come due regardless.

Darius didn't answer my question, but he smiled. "Make sure you give your lady a good Christmas." That was the trick to make it seem like no big deal. It only needed to work for that one second, to get my feet unstuck.

As I walked back to my car, I heard the latch on the door. And then the chain.

◇◇

The first snow fell three days later. I drove over to Darius's place before and after work, just to walk around the neighborhood. I could have just parked in a lawn chair in front of his place, but I figured that would attract attention.

I kept having this funny thought about jail. I'd done a night in here or there when my buddies and I had got up to it a little too much, and the times when I would still be in after I sobered up I remember how strange the passage of time became. There was no clock to look to and there was nowhere to go. It was just you and the walls. When a teacher would put me in the corner, or when my folks would put me in my room, they would always say something like, "Sit here and think about what you did."

I wondered if Darius had done something. It didn't seem possible; you'd never pick a fight with him, but he wasn't mean. He was probably the most righteous of all of us. And if he'd done something, they would have put him in jail or stripped his medals. I didn't know why that thought got into my head, but once it did I hated it. I wanted to see him to get rid of it; he could make it all vanish with just one "Shucks..." That was the first time the promise got hard.

Kayla took a job at the Best Buy for the holiday. She thought it might help us save a little and get some nicer things, and she said we could get cheap movies for people for presents and that made a lot of sense. Thanksgiving was about a week after Darius locked himself in, and as I'd hoped we had it with Kayla's folks. She talked me into a proper haircut and a button shirt, and even though I was squirming in my clothes at the table, I could tell her mom liked the look of me better.

I saw that comfort somehow pass from her into Kayla's pop, just with a little glance or noise or two. It started just with her but it ended up with both of them being more okay with me. It was the first time I got some idea of what marriage is like other than all the paperwork and the vows: for Kayla's parents, it was a shared feeling that either one of you can put something into.

They asked about Darius. Kayla and I had talked about what I should say, so I told them he had been kind of worn out by all the welcomes back, and that it made him feel like he'd had his holidays already, so he was just going to take it easy. That made sense to them and they said he had always been a humble soul.

After dinner, Kayla and her mom were in the kitchen cleaning up, and her pop came into the living room with a pair of beers. "Dinner's done so we can have these now," he said, popping one for me as he sat in the twin of the scratchy yellow chair where I was resting.

For a few sips he didn't say anything, and then finally I heard, "Kayla's a special girl." I sure agreed so I gave him a good hearty nod. He cleared his throat a whole lot and then said, "It's not quite...Christian...the way you two are together right now, but I haven't always been the best Christian either so I guess I'm trying to get over it."

"I'd never treat her bad, Mr. Gray, I hope you know."

The smallest touch of grief slid over his face, but my answer also seemed to relax him some, because he let himself smile. "I know that, son. You're all right. You work hard and you take care of her. I watched the whole pack of you grow up, and I can't say as I was sure whether you'd turn out. But I always knew she liked you. You remember that time when you were 'bout ten and six of you came back from the creek all mudded up and I yelled at you the worst?"

I chuckled. "I never forgot. I thought you were going to breathe fire on me."

Mr. Gray almost coughed up a splash of beer at that. "If I could I would have. I think it's because I knew she went down there because you were going. I couldn't see why you. You were such a little shit."

I had never known that about Kayla before. But she could be driven by thoughts that were somehow both strong and quiet at the same time, so I believed it. And he was right about me, so I chuckled again. "I guess I was."

Mr. Gray took another long sip, finishing off the can. Another wave of grief passed over his face. "Listen...if you want to come around sometime and ask me a question, I won't uh...breathe fire on you for asking it. You get me?"

I knew what he was saying and it made me feel small all over. Most days I was proud of having my own place and paying the bills and keeping my job, and all that suddenly didn't feel like so much. But the smallness didn't feel all bad; I didn't know what that meant and I didn't know what to say, so I just nodded and mumbled some thanks to him.

He needed to get out one more thing, and announced it by waving his arm vaguely while stifling a burp. "If you're gonna, though, see if you can ask it sooner rather than later. For her mother, you know?"

<><>*

The next Thursday was the first time I saw Darius's Mom outside his house. She was banging on the door and singing out, "Darius! You in there? Is my boy in there?" Then she would cinch up her coat, stomp her feet on the porch a bit to keep warm, mumble something about the lack of devotion in leaving a mother out on the porch to freeze, then start all over again with the banging.

I hesitated for a second before getting her attention. Not because I didn't know if it was what I should do, but because I didn't like that I was going to have to do it. I called out and waved to her, and when she recognized me she marched right for me. Her hair was cooked out big like she'd do when she wanted to look presentable.

"Why haven't I seen my boy in a month? Did they ship him out again? It'd be just like that Army, sending my wounded boy out again."

"No, no. He's not going out again, he's rehabbing and then he's done."

"But they'll still pay him, won't they? It wasn't his fault he got hurt like that."

"I don't really know how all that works, to be honest, ma'am. I just help him get to P.T. and around and stuff."

Her eyes got sharp. She drew her whole face into a tight, bright smile, and she touched me lightly on the arm and said, "Will you tell him to come around and see his Mama? I do miss my big, beautiful boy." The look held as long as it took me to nod, and then all of her went kind of soft again, like she had just spent all the pull-together she had. She went off, tugging at her coat.

I decided to sit on Darius's front porch for a bit. A little snow was falling and the boards were deep-chilled. At first I told myself I needed to make sure his mother didn't come back, but fifteen minutes passed and I didn't leave. I just sat, wondering if he was sleeping in there. Wondering if he was dreaming.

❊❊❊

The Christmas lights were up in town and Kayla and I went out with a couple of thermoses and walked the main drag. I didn't like the way she gave me a little extra hug when families with small kids brushed by, but I didn't say anything. Santa – really old Stan who used to run the camera store – was on top of the fire truck. It's the only big, red vehicle we have, but kids love both Santa and fire trucks so it always worked out.

I'd seen these lights every year growing up. The window displays hadn't changed; the antique store still does the manger while the ice cream place has Santa's workshop. Around age eleven I was sick of the whole thing: sick of the carolers in the bonnets and the little Scrooge show they'd put on, sick of the children lining up for Santa Stan like suckers. Darius and Kayla and the others and I would slip away from our parents and light firecrackers under the bridge or piss in the snow or pass around a stolen beer.

Now, though, something was turning; I was sorta glad it was all still there. And I was glad Kayla had worn the new pink coat she'd bought for herself. I still thought the thing was gaudy, but I could see it made her happy, and its bold color made her a new Kayla; not a different person, but also not the buddy-girl I'd run around with then.

I wondered if Darius was missing this. I know when you set out to do something hard there comes a stretch when all you have going for you is sheer stubbornness. He had to know there were Christmas cards from his mailbox sitting in a pile at my place, that folks were throwing parties, that The Wet was doing the hot cider with Yukon Jack in the special curvy glasses Josie kept in the back. He'd done without those for a couple of years because he was over, but now it was all right outside his door. The only thing stopping him from having it was him.

I caught myself looking around for him. I thought maybe he wouldn't be able to resist showing up, and that I would be able to tell him that it was okay. I kept picturing him coming over the bridge, even though that wasn't the way to his house.

But he didn't appear. I was sure it was only stubbornness, and that it had to be hurting him. I was hurting for him. Kayla asked me what was on my mind, and I told her I was thinking about what to buy my folks for Christmas. I think she knew I was lying.

◇◇

A lot of the men liked to gather at The Wet on Christmas Eve, have a few drinks, and keep their women waiting a bit. They didn't say out loud that's what the tradition was, but as soon as a man settled down with someone he seemed to figure it out. Kayla was pulling double-pay to work the last shift at the Best Buy so I knew it was nothing off me to stop in.

All the bundled up people crowded into each other. Faces were loose and happy. Some of the boys had put money together to get presents for Josie and her girls. I sat at the back corner table, alone at first, though lot of folks tipped their glasses on the way by.

Jake Sherrill, whose brother works at the Beebe garage, came out of the men's room; he trailed a hand along the wall as he walked for balance. He passed me by, then stopped, wobbled for a second, and turned to look at me.

"Where's he at?" he asked with a slack grin. Jake and I had scrapped some when we were younger, but he'd never started any business while Darius was around. I looked back at the bar to see what group he was hanging with, but nobody seemed to be looking for him, so I was stuck with him until he wanted to do something else.

"He's just healing up."

Jake gave a big stupid shrug. "Well what's that all about? He was healed fine enough to come around here a while ago." He sauntered over and put his beer in the middle of the table like to claim it. "Want to know what I hear? I hear he pisses himself. I hear he pisses himself if he sees his own shadow now."

I tasted acid in my mouth but I kept my seat. "Ain't true."

He leaned in now and breathed stink all over me. "I hear you go over to his house every day to change his big man diaper."

God help me it wasn't a clean fight or a long one, but I bet you anything I gave Jake Sherrill worse than he gave me.

⁕⁕⁕

Kayla found me groaning in the dark with a bag of frozen corn over one eye. There had been three cops at The Wet, but they were off-duty, so while it was in their nature to break things up and settle the room, they didn't think it was worth turning into official business. They made me and Jake shake hands, straighten up, and agree to split the damages before they let us go. We agreed to it. Being a deadbeat at The Wet would be worse than being in front of a judge; Jake and I knew that drunk or sober. I was only a beer-and-a-half in when it went down so I drove myself home. My hands hurt worst of all. I was proud of that.

Kayla made a disapproving sound, but she was tired from work so she just curled up there next to me on the couch, tucking into any unbruised spot she could find. "They don't get it," I said quietly. "They don't get what he's doing."

"Honey, you said you don't get what he's doing."

I looked at our little Christmas tree, the only light in the room other than the stars and the moon coming through the window. "Doesn't matter if I don't get it. Not my job."

She tipped up her head, and although I could barely see I knew which face she was making. "Sometimes I don't know if you're the best friend a person could want or the worst."

I held onto her tight. Just about anyone else saying that, I would have heard an insult.

❋❋❋

After the New Year I started spending more time at Darius' place. It was evil cold but there was something comfortable about the routine. I'd shovel the snow off the drive, check the gutters and the pipes, that kind of thing. I didn't put my ear to the door or windows; that felt rude.

His mother came by again, grumpy and jumpy this time. She had her mind set on seeing him. I wasn't going to put my hands on her, but I didn't like the thought of her making a scene big enough to bring the cops around. It was Darius's property: they'd insist on talking to him, and that would scotch the whole thing.

Eventually I made up some story that he had a girl in there, and she was an officer, so they couldn't be caught fraternizing. I guess that hit her in just the right spot, because she finally looked at me instead of the house. "Is that right?" she said, and grinned. "My boy is a RASCAL!" Then she called out in a friendly, taunting way. "You hear that, Darius? You are a rascal! And make that double since you aren't coming around to see your momma. I'll be back again but you treat her right now, you hear?"

Not long after she left, I happened to look up and I saw smoke coming out the chimney. Darius was in there. He was keeping himself warm, or cooking up beans, or something. It didn't matter. He was in there.

❖❖

I went over to my dad's place and dug our old camping gear out of the garage. With a good sleeping bag and a space heater to go with the tent and the cot, I thought I might hazard the night in Darius's backyard.

My dad flipped on the garage light and caught me in there. He was in a robe and had about four days' gray stubble, and his hair was all matted down. It made me think he hadn't been working. He didn't say anything, just nodded and squinted in my direction.

I told him what I was looking for, and he jerked his head towards where the cot was living, behind a pile of rusted lawn chairs. As I tugged it out, he finally spoke.

"Going fishing?"

I made up a story about how me and Kayla were looking to go up to the mountains when the weather warmed up some, and how I wanted to see what we could scrounge together now so I'd know what to save for. My gut pinched after I said that. What was it about what I was doing that I was having to lie to so many folks? I'd told all kinds of lies: little ones, tall tales, fish stories, whoppers. Mostly the scared ones you told when you got caught doing what you shouldn't. I felt bad about them as much as the next person...but like the next person, it didn't stop me from another.

This lying felt different, though. I knew why I was telling them – the more people who knew what Darius was up to, the more they'd want to get themselves involved in it, mostly to stop him. That's how Kayla had reacted. Who knew if they actually could help him, but they'd want to do it anyway. There are certain kinds of sadnesses that people feel like they have to show everyone they're doing something about, even if it's just to yap their opinion or piss all over it like Jake Sherrill did. The thought that they could help the most by standing back and letting Darius try was so backwards that they wouldn't have been able to imagine it.

Lying made everyone's life easier, but I still didn't like that I had to do it. I didn't like what it said about folks.

∗◦∗

Kayla and I got into a fight when I told her I was going out to sleep at Darius's. Well, not a fight. It was an argument, though, a real bellower. It's not that she thought I was stepping out on her, and it's true that she didn't like sleeping alone in our bed, but that wasn't the big deal either. It was a kind of jealousy, I guess. She knew this was important but didn't see how sleeping out there was necessary. I said that half of every day was night, and more so in winter, and that meant if something was going to happen it was at least as likely to happen at night. Weather could break a window, an animal could slip in; so many things could happen.

I think she was feeling anxious. It was dark so early, and she'd stopped the Best Buy job and was back to just those few hours a week she put in at the school. She didn't want to just be alone in the evenings with the TV. I told her she should go out with her girlfriends and she said that most of them were pregnant; I took that as a dig and got extra steamed with her. When I'm scrapping with a guy, there comes a point pretty quick when words make so little sense that you just go to the fists kind of by mutual agreement. That isn't right with your girl, but I knew pretty much everything we were saying didn't make any more sense than the noises that come out of a backed-up cat. But we were saying it, and we couldn't seem to stop.

I stormed out, camping gear and all. I'd never done that to her before. Never in all our lives.

❋❋❋

I'd forgotten the sound a cold wind makes scraping across the walls of a tent. It whips and snaps and it never stops. I had pitched the tent pretty near the back wall of Darius' house just to have shelter on that side, but that wasn't too much relief. I could see more chimney smoke, and I thought how sweet it would be to just be in there: Darius and me with a couple of whiskeys in front of the fire. I'd tell him about the fight between Kayla and me, and he'd chuckle and shrug it off and tell some funny story about something we all got up to when we were little. All it would take would be an hour or so of that and I could go home to her and make it all better.

I didn't realize how hard it would be, to be pressed right up against his home, knowing he was in there, and not to go inside. I thought about the fire, the fire, the fire, and as I slouched over the heater and shivered I felt mad that he would ask this of me. He knew I'd be the one who'd do this for him, and do it the way he wanted, but that didn't make it righteous. Not any way around. What was he doing in there? Sleeping, crying, getting fat, pulling it? Was he bored? Nuts? When was he coming out?

I rocked back and forth over the edge of sleep that night, sometimes waking and sometimes dreaming, and the night seemed to stretch out for a lifetime. I think I dreamed about a light, the light I imagined the sun made out in the kind of desert where Darius had been. It hurt, how white that light was, just searing bright, punching through everything. And the ground was hot. Shit, it was cooking me.

When I would rock back awake the cold would get me again and it was harsh, like being slapped by sharp ice. I feared the heat from my dream, but craved it, too.

Voices woke me, an urgent muttering coming from out around the house. I didn't know what time it was but the clouds covered the moon and the wind had gone still. I slipped on my boots and my coat, and crunched the fresh snow in careful steps as I made my way around the side.

I saw three dark bundles of coats and gloves, smoke of their breath illuminated in the light cast by the streetlamp. One was kneeling by the front door, jiggling the handle, while the other two had moved along the porch to the window. One of those was holding a rock, standing very still, while the other...I didn't need words, I knew the conversation just from the way they stood. The one with the rock was making up his mind whether he was going to break that window. The one next to him was egging him on. The one at the lock was trying to let the air out of the situation by trying the door again. But it wasn't going to work. The rock was going to win the argument. One way or another, they were going into his house.

I pulled myself onto the porch and roared at them. The one at the door just jackrabbited at the first sound. The one with the rock kind of looked down at it for a second, then at me, and then he dropped it and took off.

I tackled the third one on the porch. I hadn't managed words yet, just this crazy cry of hurt and fury. I sat on the would-be-intruder, put my fists up, and got ready to beat the man underneath me until he would never even think of coming back. I pulled the scarf off his face, and that's when I realized that it was a kid. Sixteen maybe, and that was giving him credit. He had braces on his teeth and show-off fuzz on his cheeks, and he was looking at me like I was every mugger and rapist and derelict he'd ever been warned about, like I was a lion that was going to eat him.

He shivered and gulped and his whole body below the neck was limp. Half of him was feeling this was the fight for his life, and the other half was too shocked to fight it. His so-called friends were long gone.

I shouted as I pushed him into the porch boards. "What are you doing?" It was all I could say, over and over. And all he could say was, "Nothing! I'm not doing anything!" He was whimpering now, and I could see the shame on him for it.

I got off him, jerking my head at the street and growling to tell him to leave now. He was too scared to run at first. He was so ready to deserve a beating, and in some ways running away is worse than any black eye or broken bone. But when I made to jump at him again he scrambled and ran, falling and crawling when he had to, off through the snow.

I gulped at the air and pounded the hard, freezing wood of the porch in anger at both myself and the kids. I hadn't asked them why they were there. Did they know he was in there? Were they trying to rob the place? Had they heard stories and just couldn't help talk themselves into seeing for themselves? Or were they just goddamn bored enough that putting a rock through someone's window sounded better than any other idea?

I stood outside Darius's door for a long time. I felt like this had to be the moment – I had to knock, I had to tell him it was me, tell him that something had happened. I wanted to ask him if he was okay. That was the single hardest moment of the promise. My hand hovered in the air in front of the door. I prayed that he would just open it and take this burden off me.

But he didn't. The night went still again, and it was just me and the heat in my blood, alone and hurting.

I left the tent there and went home. I slipped into the bed next to Kayla, and held her, and told her that we ought to get married.

✷✧✷

It was a long, horrible gray January, and that gray gobbled up most of February, too. The cold kept most everybody indoors, with exceptions for work, family, or The Wet. I didn't camp out at Darius's again, but I still made my rounds before and after work. People had stopped asking about him. It was almost like he had gone overseas again; someone might mention his name telling some story, but the talk would peter out quick, like it was bad luck to say his name out loud before he came back to us.

Kayla and I gave people plenty to talk about, though. A few folk were whispering that she had to be knocked up for the announcement to be so sudden. But Kayla's family was thrilled that we wanted to get hitched, and she spent a lot of time with her mother, going over pictures and making invitation lists. They hauled out her mother's old wedding dress, and I could tell from the first that they were never, ever going to use it, because it had gone yellow and was way too big. But they spent hours fussing over it and talking about what they could do with it, and her Dad convinced me that this was a blessing and we should just leave them to it.

One night at The Wet after a couple of beers I looked around and it seemed like people were so huddled up cold that they weren't talking to each other. Suddenly I didn't like that. Without telling anyone I slipped down the long hallway to the bathrooms, only I went past them to where the furnace knob was around the corner. Feeling like I was stealing something, I turned it up high, high enough to hear the short little roar of the furnace going to work.

I went back to sit, and it got toasty in there, hot enough that people were peeling off their sweaters. Just like I'd hoped, people brightened up and chatted and hugged each other more. Maybe it would be bad for their gas bill, but I bought a glass of whiskey, climbed up on a stool, and used my right as a newly-engaged man to propose a toast to love and friendship. The crowd purchased many more drinks, so I think I balanced the books for The Wet by that.

✕◇✕

The afternoon of the first day of March, I left work grateful for the fact that I finally wasn't completely freezing my ass off. It hadn't snowed for a week, and while the dirty wet slush still smothered the sidewalks, and the hard, shoveled packs still clumped up against walls, the wind had calmed, and when the sky did clear for the sun it didn't feel so barren and stark. You could feel some warmth from it. It was a long way to spring, but a respite from punishment is its own pleasure.

At Darius' house, I scooped up the paper, grabbed the mail, and walked around to look at the pipes and the back windows and door. My daily route had worn a path around his house, enough that you could see the scrabbly graveyard of a lawn underneath the snow, waiting to revive.

I had gotten used to thinking over a lot during these walks. I'd trudge and look around and just mull on stuff. I had a whole list of people that had pissed me off who I imagined telling off. And I thought about how I didn't know if I was doing the right thing getting married. I didn't know if I should be making more money. I didn't know if I was a bad son. I didn't know what I would have done out there on that hot street Darius had been walking down when that mine blew up; if I'd have just given in to the flames or gutted it out.

I never figured out any of what I didn't know, but somehow by the time I was done I was more okay with it.

I got back around to the front of the house and was fixed to leave. I took one last look back, and there was the front door, open. An open door is such a regular thing, but Darius' had been closed for so long that it took me a bit to believe it. Had anyone had the time or the balls to break in with my car in the driveway, with me walking around the house?

I could just make out the shape of a man slumped against the door frame, facing out at me with a dark house behind him. Panic filled me and I ran to the porch steps.

It was Darius, weak but standing. He was wrapped up in blankets, looking at me with squinting eyes. His lip shook a little and I heard a rattle of breath, but he didn't speak.

I took two quick steps towards him to pick him up and embrace him, but his eyes widened in fright. He looked like he wasn't sure I was there. "It's me, man," I said. He didn't say anything. He just turned, slowly, and shuffled back inside.

I came in behind him. No lights were on anywhere. The smell of the place hit me – must and garbage. The couch in the living room had been dragged over towards the fireplace, and a massive pile of blankets and bed comforters lived on it. A neat stack of garbage bags dominated one half of the kitchen; the other was a minefield of eaten-out cans kicked into a haphazard pile, drawing in bugs. There was no way to know if Darius had started out organized and then become this bitter scrounger, if it were the other way, or even if he changed from hour to hour.

Nothing was left on the walls. Pictures, clocks, calendars, his ribbons case: they'd all been taken down. Books were all around in piles, and by each pile was a flashlight.

He was looking down at the couch, bent half over it. "You want help getting down?" I asked. He didn't answer, so I came in close anyway, tried to push myself up under his arm so he could rest his weight. He took the help, lowered himself down, sighing and settling. He sounded like the old men I knew, who made a hundred little quiet cries a day from all the parts of their bodies that had come to hurting.

"Can you talk?"

His eyes fixed on me and he cocked his head like he wasn't sure himself. Then his head dropped, at first I thought in sadness – then I saw him looking at the floor around him. I saw a big water bottle on the floor there, on its side like it had been dropped. I quickly picked it up, unscrewed the cap, and brought it towards him slowly. Panic flashed in his eyes as regularly as a heartbeat.

One hand came up under the bottle as I held it to his lips. I let him take that bit of the weight, though I couldn't swear he would have been able to take it all. I heard the water wash around in his throat as he swallowed and coughed. Finally he gave a little nod as if to say enough, and I backed up a couple of steps and squatted so I wouldn't be looking down on him.

His lips opened and shut a couple of times, as if they needed the practice, and at last he spoke. "Yeah, I can talk." He shrugged himself up in the chair and looked around the room with disgust. Then he looked back down at the floor, and this time it was sad. "Thanks man. Hoped it was you."

In all the years I've run with Darius, there's one thing that's been true: so simple true I hadn't even seen it. It had taken Kayla to point it out to me, not long after she and I got serious. We were in the back of Chuckie Ruck's van in the brush off the end of Pipestone Road when she said it. She'd had two beers, which was always enough to make her silly. She said, "You make him laugh. It's your job. Whenever you don't know what to do, you try to make him laugh."

It seemed like a long time since we'd been young, but I was still doing it. "So I can take off if you want, but I got to tell you, the groundhog didn't see his shadow, so winter's done ya lazy ass."

Darius groaned, but before he could finish the sound it turned and became more of a grumble, tired but warm. "That so?" he replied. "You wouldn't lie to me?" I shook my head, grinning.

He settled back in the chair again for a moment, gathering himself. "Oatmeal. I want about five pounds of hot oatmeal."

"I've got some back at home."

"No, man. Kayla shouldn't see me like this. You know the truck stop we pass to and from PT?" I nodded right away – it was about twenty miles down the road; a place nobody in town went. "That's where I want to go. Am I stealing you away from her?"

"I've got some credit with her right now. Told her I'd marry her."

His eyes got wet and I saw the first thing that looked like a smile. "Course you did. Now, before I threaten to beat you if you don't make me best man, help me get to the latrine."

⁂

The drive to the truck stop was silent. The bare trees in the dusk whipped alongside the truck like a rippling curtain. All Darius's clothes hung differently on him: his chest had shrunk and his skin had drooped under his jaw and he had a small, soft belly now. It looked like his whole body had just surrendered toward the ground. He watched out the window and there were still moments of that strange terror I'd glimpsed when he'd first come out of his den.

We found the truck stop; it glowed from far away. Rigs growled and steamed in the parking lot, and inside the drivers lined up at the counter with their coffees. "Not ready for a cup," Darius sighed, "but I love that smell."

Nobody gave him a second glance in our booth by the window; the scarred half of his head was turned to the outside. The path we were on felt right – the porch steps had been a challenge, and he had stared at his street lamp for a long time, like he mistook it for the sun, but he had made it out, and soon he would have food. There was so much I was desperate to hear him say, though, and I didn't know how to start.

The waitress came. I asked for turkey hash and he asked for his oatmeal. "And a milk," he said. "Wait!" he stopped the waitress. "Chocolate milk." When she left, he said to me with the seriousness of death, "Been dreaming of chocolate milk, man."

"Do you know what day it is?" I asked.

He just shook his head. "Just heard you outside. I got to know that sound. Morning and night – you tromping through the snow around the house, on patrol. Took a lot to make it to the door."

We talked about easier stuff for a while: stuff that had come in the mail, how the holidays had gone for me and Kayla. The oatmeal came and he started to scoop it down, and he chugged his first chocolate milk before the waitress could even turn on her heel.

"You look different," he said to me. I couldn't figure what he meant by that. He was the one looked different. He was so changed that I still felt anxious to see him.

This time he was able to make it to the can on his own. He was in for a while but I didn't worry. I called Kayla, gave her the latest. She wanted to see him as soon as possible.

When Darius came back there was something decisive in the way he dropped back into his seat. I straightened up. He looked me in the eyes, and he could see he had my attention. For a second he looked away, then took the menu out again and mumbled, "Wonder if I'm ready for fried chicken...how bad could it hurt?"

Then he slapped the menu back down and looked at me clear and strong. He pointed at the scarred side of his head. "You know what this is?"

I didn't know how to answer, so I just said, "From the mine, yeah?"

"Yeah. Goddamn column of hellfire opened up in front of me. Killed some good men. Docs on the base tell me that I'm seeing that hellfire over and over again, reliving it. Except I don't. Sure, I'll look at it sometimes, like the way you rub something to see if it still hurts, and it does. Shit it does. But I don't think it bothers me like they keep saying it does.

"Thing is…the reason my scars look this way is that fire. It melted my helmet. The plastic melted into my skull. My goddamned helmet became a part of my head, for life, man. Do you see how strange that is? I haven't stopped thinking about that since the doctor told me."

And the way he said it I could see that it was strange, the most bottomless kind of strange. He went on, his eyes welling up. "I'm not a soldier anymore. But if I'm not a soldier, how come I've got a helmet on? How come?" He looked up for a moment, searching up there for I don't know what, and kept on. "I don't know how to say this, but when you talked about a bear sleeping through winter, I heard the strangest voice in my head. And it said 'maybe I'm a bear.' And that was the first time in months I'd thought I could be anything else. So I suddenly just had to know if I could be a bear."

And now his head fell into his palms, and he shuddered. "So damn stupid. So stupid. Look at me now. Can barely walk on my own."

I felt a quiet and cavernous sense of doubt. All winter I'd told myself that whatever Darius was doing, it was what he needed to get better. But to look at him, to hear him now, I didn't know if he had broken through or just broke.

A thousand thoughts ran through my head, wanting action. All at the same time I wanted to rage in wondering what it was all about, to tell him his idea was stupid, to tell him his idea was perfect, to cry with him, to punch him in the jaw for leaving me to worry in the cold for so long. Instead, I just waited until his tearful heaves stopped, and thought back to that night in the Wet when he'd pounded the table and howled and I'd laughed so hard. And I remembered what had brought it all on. "You know Darius, I've never heard anyone else use the expression 'hunt you like a slow bear.' Where'd you get that from?"

I could see him stretch far back in his memory, pulling on his consciousness like a rubber band. The energy of a great vibration filled him and played on his face, as if in finding the answer his thoughts had come rocketing back past all the glories and miseries that had passed in-between so as to make them a blur. I prayed that it had gone past the now and far into the future of his life, so that he could remember he had one waiting for him.

He shrugged his shoulders and suddenly gave the most beautiful easy chuckle. "I think it was just this one time my daddy and me were watching some nature show. I had to be about five or six. He loved the nature shows, but I asked him why we never saw any film of a bear running. Nature shows always have the animals running, but the bears always just trudge around, you know? So I ask him, and he says 'I don't know, but maybe that explains how something that big can end up as a rug.' That was a pretty awful thought, but it was kind of funny, too. After that, if we saw a bear on a nature show we'd shout 'Run, bear, run!' I took it real serious, man."

"That's it?" I said, having this funny feeling like I'd been turned inside-out. "Run, bear, run?"

"That's it," said Darius, and he picked up the menu again. "God-damn, now I really do want some meat."

❊❖❊

II. THE PASSAGE

"At night, when the objective world has slunk back into its cavern and left dreamers to their own, there come inspirations and capabilities impossible at any less magical and quiet hour. "
– H.P. Lovecraft

"Be careful what you water your dreams with."
– Lao Tzu

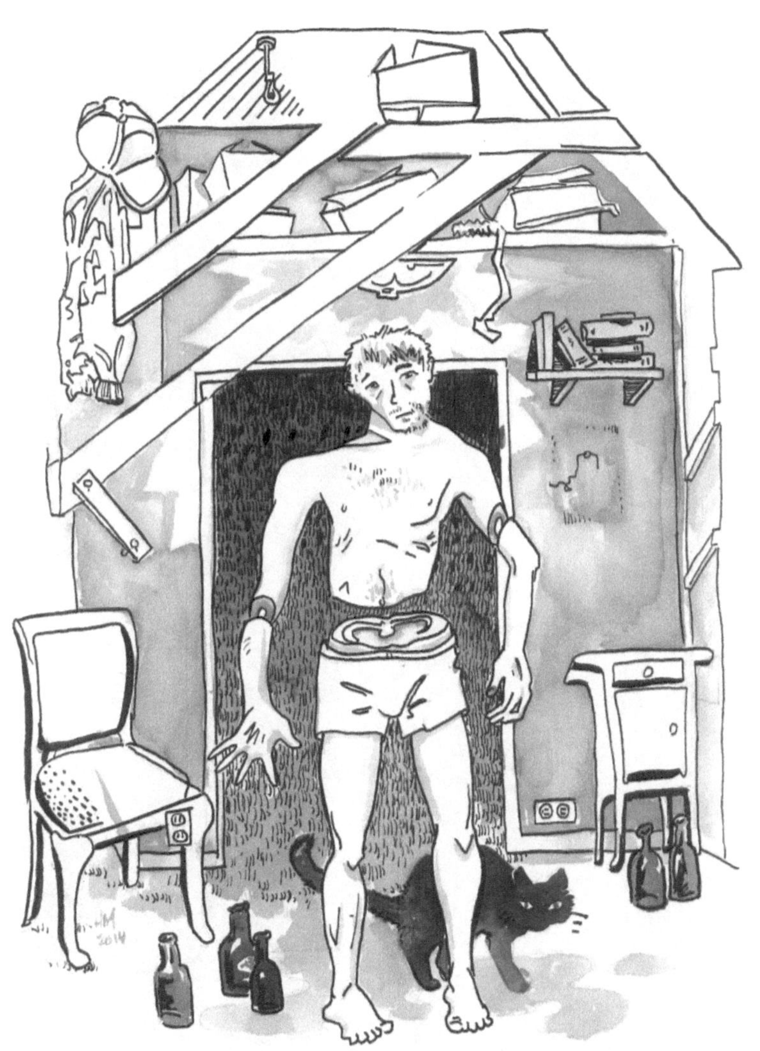

THE STARING MAN

It was 2:30 in the a.m. when the naked people ran through the lobby. Maurice was so astonished that they were past the front desk before he could even register it happening. Six of them – all men. One of them was waving an unshucked ear of corn.

He had no time at all to go through all the procedures in the manual in order to decide if one accommodated such an event. So Maurice could only stare while the six naked men, whooping and jabbering, jogged past the elevators, and then through the breakfast lounge, before pushing their way out a fire exit at the back.

A high, panicked bell clattered. Still gaping, Maurice helplessly rewound his brain to decide whether or not he had actually seen – things. He squinted, tried to paint black spots into his memory to censor that idea, but it was useless; so he focused on willing the whole event away.

As the night manager, Maurice was very sure it was his job to do something. The alarm bell was an easy first step. Fishing the appropriate key off the ring at his belt, he crossed the lobby to the door, shut it, and de-activated the alarm. Already his phone was ringing, and once he pacified the guest on the phone, Maurice at last had the time to feel affronted. This was a respectable hotel. He knew for a fact that their laundry standards were far more stringent than any of those motels off the highway three miles west, and more than once it had served as an alternate site for small conventions crowded out of the Holiday Inn over on the backside of the airport.

He had worked there for twelve years, and he felt a parental investment in the place. This spectacle worried him. He wondered if it portended something. A place could get a reputation quickly. He found his eyes darting to the wide glass front doors, hoping to get advance warning of any other naked mobs.

Was it really just something rowdy young men had come up with on their own? Why? It seemed to Maurice like these days people did things like this so they could get on the Internet. Or people did them and then ended up on the Internet whether they wanted to or not. He knew the Internet worked one of those ways but he didn't spend much time with it. The security cameras had probably captured the incident, but he didn't know enough about the security apparatus to know if there was a risk of it leaking out onto the Internet from there. He was reasonably confident that couldn't happen: the system hadn't been updated in a while.

Then Maurice remembered he was not the only witness. And so he turned his attention back to the thing that had been distracting him all night: the man sitting in the plastic chair by the tourist brochures. He had been there since Maurice clocked in five hours before – an older gentleman, broad in the chest, gray on the head, dressed in a faded tweed suit with a vest. He sat with impeccable posture, and in all those hours had not moved to any noticeable degree. He just sat, staring straight ahead. Whenever he had no responsibilities to attend to, Maurice found himself wondering about this man.

His phone rang, and he answered. "Front desk?" The tone he used was one he had practiced many, many times, and he thought it conveyed the perfect amount of professionalism and courtesy at a volume appropriate for nighttime.

"How many hours?" The guest on the other end asked. The voice dragged, like an old record played too slow.

"Excuse me?"

"How many hours before the flight?"

Sleep walkers were more common than sleep callers, but both happened from time to time.

"I'm sorry, I don't have that information."

"Am I getting a meal?"

"I'm sure you will, sir."

"Make sure I get a meal." And with a click, the conversation ended.

Maurice replaced the phone, stretched his shoulders back and heard three little cracks drip down his spine. Two years ago it had only been two. Or was it three years ago?

He felt his belly unconsciously for a moment – his uniform still fit and he took pride in that. He brushed lint off the counter, then caught himself casting a worried eye on the fire exit.

In two hours he would vacuum. The cleaning crew had already come and gone, but he felt that a last run with the vacuum a little before sunup gave the carpet a freshness in the morning. Respectable establishments cared about the little things. Maurice believed strongly in that.

Again he looked at the old man. His hands were propped on top of a cane; it seemed to bear a little weight, keeping him balanced and still. Maurice could see now that the man was leaning slightly forward, as if in anticipation. Still relaxed, still dignified, but looking forward to something. And yet all that was in front of him was the opposite wall.

The lobby had interesting walls – Maurice had appreciated this from the start. Wood columns with miles of grain lines, paint refreshed every other year. But Maurice was very confident that the man wasn't even looking at the walls – his eyes seemed focused on some point far beyond them, like he could see into the room on the other side with the ice machine, and something exciting was happening in there.

The elevator hummed. By the length of the sound Maurice guessed it came from the fourth floor. He made sure not to be staring directly at it when it returned to the lobby and opened. People found that distressing.

A man, fully dressed in a crisp, classy suit, emerged, and strode confidently up to the counter. "Evening!" he declared with confidence.

"Good evening, sir. How can I help you?"

"Have you got any ear plugs back there?"

Maurice turned to the drawer on his right. "Of course. Is there noise that's bothering you?" He found a package of foam earplugs, placed them neatly on the counter, and then slid them towards the gentleman with one finger.

The man in the suit picked them up and slipped them in a side pocket: "Nothing like that. But I can't sleep without the TV on, and it's loud."

Maurice frowned; it was impolite to point out the obvious to a guest, but he couldn't help himself. "Couldn't you turn the television volume down?"

The man shook his head. "No, no, that wouldn't work at all. I appreciate the help. You have a good night!" And with that, he walked right out the lobby doors into the night.

Maurice heard the man's heels clicking away on the pavement. He didn't understand it at all.

Flustered, he decided to fill out the cleaning assignment sheet early. Normally he waited to see if there were any late night arrivals (the latest check-in he had ever done was 4:30 a.m.), or any signs of possible incidents that would require extra attention, but for once he thought it would be no great loss to record some observations early.

There were no large parties booked, and the few young guests seemed harmless enough. Two were a couple obviously slipping away from their parents for the night. Maurice used to feel slightly wicked checking such people in, but had gradually preferred to avoid confrontation over it. If they both wanted to be there, it was a safer, more comfortable environment than in one of those motels; or, god forbid, in a truck on some dark road. At least there was affection involved, rather than the chilly commerce he saw happen occasionally.

He snuck another glance at the old man. Had a foot shifted forward slightly? Was his head tilted more to one side? It was difficult to tell from Maurice's vantage point. There, did the fingers flex in their grip on top of the cane?

Maurice remembered some program from television about people in the Far East who would sit still for days on end, just thinking about big, spiritual things. Perhaps this old man was a traveler who had lived among them – except that Maurice was very sure those Eastern people did it with their eyes closed.

He's just asleep, Maurice thought. Then: *No, he's dead!* This would be a whole other category of problem, and Maurice hated the thought of it. It wasn't the possibility of seeing death up close, or knowing that it would be his responsibility to take action about it that bothered him, but what did it say that not only might he have a corpse in his lobby, but he had let it sit there for hours as people walked by going about their business?

The phone rang again. "Front desk?"

"When is the sun coming up?"

Maurice thought back to the end of his last couple of shifts. "About 5:50, I would guess."

"Can I see it out my window or do I have to go outside?"

Maurice referred to the room number and double-checked his map of the hotel. "The sun will be rising on the opposite side of the hotel, sir."

"Huh. Can I move rooms? It's very important."

Maurice squinted, feeling a tingle grow behind his eyes as he tried his best to be of service. "If your room is unsatisfying, you are welcome to come down to the lobby and we can see if there's an available room that meets your needs."

"Oh, I thought I could just, like, go across the hall and you could open the door with a button or something. Can't you do that?"

"No, I'm afraid there is no such button at this hotel."

"Should I knock on some doors, maybe? Maybe if I explain it to someone they'll let me stay with them."

Maurice let his voice become stern, and slightly louder. "I'll have to ask for you to not do that, so as not to disturb other guests."

"Okay. It's important, though."

The tingling spread – it was almost like his head was going to sleep like a dead limb. "All I can suggest, sir, is that you come to the front desk."

"Never mind." And the man hung up. Maurice dearly hoped that would be the end of that affair.

Normally Maurice valued the quiet of the night shift. The occasional car passing on the highway, the little hums and pops he recognized in the building. Sometimes he even imagined he could hear all the way down the hallway to the lapping of the indoor pool. But tonight the silence wore at him.

He reached for a crossword puzzle. He normally didn't afford himself diversions except during scheduled breaks, but he felt nervous, and he was the only authority in the place. He could always stuff it under the counter if another employee passed through. But he couldn't answer a single clue; all of them seemed to defy reasoning. A twelve-letter synonym for cat? A Latin phrase for "call the fire department"?

Maurice slapped the puzzle back down on the counter. The old man in the chair didn't flinch.

At last, Maurice stepped out from behind the counter. *I am the night manager,* he told himself, stretching his back once again. *The lobby is my business.* He walked up to the old man, stopping by his left shoulder; walking directly towards someone's face could be taken as aggressive.

"Excuse me...excuse me, sir?" The old man didn't respond, but Maurice could see the subtle rise and fall of slow breathing; so the man was indeed alive.

Only after he raised his voice and repeated himself did the man blink and turn his head to face him. The motion was quick and smooth, and the man regarded Maurice with a wide grin and twinkling eyes. "Yes?"

Maurice was rather staggered that the man had actually moved. He realized he hadn't planned for that happening.

"Um...well, I'm the night manager here, my name is Maurice, and I was wondering if you are a registered guest?"

The old man's face flushed, and he chuckled. "No, good Maurice, I am not. I'm sorry if I'm creating any inconvenience for you."

The answer was polite, but not good enough. "Oh, you haven't made any disturbance at all. But I do have to ask if you have anywhere you can go."

"I do, I do. I have a grand house up on the hill. Worked all my life for it. But I do hope you will allow me to finish before I leave."

"Finish what, if you don't mind me asking?"

"I don't mind at all, good Maurice. I'm shedding!"

"Excuse me?"

"I'm shedding a layer. It only happens a few times in our lives, you know, when we really change over into the next stage. Like butterflies."

Maurice thought very hard about the smartest television programs he had ever seen, and the smartest magazines he had ever read, but he had to admit he had never heard of this. "Does it, um, take long?"

"Oh, several hours at least. There were times in my life when I was hustling about so much that I didn't even pay attention to it, and others where I had become so dull that even when it happened I couldn't feel it, just because I didn't believe I could feel it. Do you understand that?"

Maurice nodded, though he honestly hadn't stopped being hung up on the word "shedding" long enough to grasp anything else.

The old man continued. "Nowadays when it happens, I just like to make myself comfortable and really feel every bit of it. I was around the corner when I felt it coming on, and I don't know that I have many left in me, so I thought I should quickly find some pleasant and comfortable place to let it happen."

Maurice straightened with pride at the compliment to his lobby. "If it's as you say, I'm flattered you chose us. Will it take much longer, do you think?"

"No, not long now. Most of the old me has already flaked away to the floor. But don't worry – you won't have to vacuum it!" He chuckled again, and his grin seemed to grow. "So, you don't mind if I...?" He let the question stay open.

Maurice was still confounded by every premise of the conversation, and yet the man had complimented the lobby. He couldn't put the man out on the street after that. So, straightening his uniform, he gave a little nod and said, "Please, enjoy the rest of your stay. Coffee begins brewing at 5:00 if you're still here."

The old man gave a final grin. "Such a kind offer. I may well need it!" And, with no further words, he turned his head away, took a deep breath, and settled back into his old pose, staring ahead at some point out beyond the wall.

As Maurice returned to the front desk, he saw something he had missed earlier – the ear of corn one of the naked people had carried. It had dropped by the potted plant that stood near the entrance to the breakfast area.

He carried it with him back to the desk, but some impulse prevented him from throwing it away. He set it on the counter and looked at it. The quiet grew comfortable again, and soon he lost track of how long he had been staring at the corn.

✻✻✻

THE CULLING OF THE BEIGE

If there was one thing she was sick of, it was these dweeb assholes in their blue-button shirts and khakis. They drank together in clusters – consultants, software engineers, tech support people. Pink men with puffy little faces and puffy little stomachs, phones clipped to their belts, night after night shuffling meekly into her bar. Why did they all have to order light beer, or, when their company had a good day and they finally felt the smallest drip of testosterone in the blood, whatever cheap import was on the ascent that year? Why, when so many hadn't yet crested thirty-five, did they seem so sedate and settled? And why did they all have to wear that outfit: blue above the waist – a crisp, medium-to-dark blue – and below the waist, beige? Wherefore beige?

Harmony hadn't wanted to hate these men. Not one of them had ever done her wrong. They passed through the hotel for a day or two, and in the evening they'd make non-threatening conversation at an easy volume, leave at a sensible hour, tip reliably. Then, she imagined, they'd fly coach class seats on an average airline home, and maybe those outfits weren't really separate pieces, but peeled off all in one like a daytime skin, and they removed them, and turned their tasteful lamp discreetly off and made adequate love to their acceptable wives.

Fuck.

Harmony had taken the job because she was good at mixing drinks, and because at a posh stop like this she was less likely to end up mixing drinks for jackasses like, well, the one she'd been married to for five years. But these clogging, inoffensive, satisfied-with-their-lot men bothered her. Their immaculate and unchallenging politeness affronted her, disrespected her.

Some nights there would be only one or two. But then some convention would come to town, and the bar would spill over with them, their blabber full of numbers and acronyms and careful laughs, and those were the nights when the fabric of her shirt itched the worst, when she could feel the waistband of her prim black vest digging into her sides.

She practiced squinting. Harmony found this a useful way to wile away the hours. Just squint and let the dark corners of the room swell, let the lights blur outward and hide the khakied men in their coronas. Who needed open eyes for this job? They'd never order anything complicated anyway. They'd never need a round of three-layer shots and a girl who knew how to serve them with a little sass.

There were four tables of them, tonight, a high volume with no convention to speak of. She washed glasses and squinted with all her might. The song on the radio was the song that had played in the tattoo parlor the day she'd had a lyre etched into the small of her back. Baseball played on the TV, and the tension was boiling with only two or three thousand games left in the season...

And then there was a great cracking sound: splintered wood, shattered glass, the hwhooshing of a fierce wind, and screams.

Harmony opened her eyes.

Table #4, by the pillar, was collapsing in on itself, as if a tiny black hole had opened up in the centerpiece. No, the hole was in the floor. A perfect black circle. The table, the bottles of light beer, the coasters, the pretzels, they were being sucked down into this hole.

The men in the blue-button shirts and khakis, they were also being sucked down into the hole.

They clawed and strained, digging their nails into the tasteful carpet, praying for a sudden usefulness in their biceps. Praying to Jesus or the 1-800 help line to pull them from this abyss. Their eyes popped and their tongues flailed, but they couldn't save themselves. Quick as you please, they and all their belongings vanished into the depths.

No one in the bar turned a head. No manager scurried in to soothe nerves. No nerves needed soothing. There were no special bulletins on the television about recently-discovered tears in the fabric of reality. The men were just gone.

The table under the ugly painting of hunters was the next to go. The group here had an especially fat one in their midst; his shirt could have tented Boy Scouts. Again the table crushed itself, again the hole in the ground, again that futile struggle for life, every wireless device on their person useless to them now. Over in seconds, and no remarks from the crowd.

A woman who may or may not have been an expensive prostitute casually ordered a Southern Comfort, to be charged to the gentleman's tab.

Harmony wondered if those sucking voids in the floor should be roped off.

She was still trying to summon up the appropriate levels of shock and pity when the other two tables of pink-blue-beige men dropped one after the other. Each time, after the cacophony, the final sound of each collapse was a punctual *thwip!*, like space and time were sucking up a strand of spaghetti. Wherever the holes went, they were too deep to remember any screams.

The song on the radio switched to something soothing, with horns.

The holes in the floor closed up, leaving nothing but clean wood and carpet.

Harmony searched every pair of eyes in the room for another witness. But everyone droned on with their conversations and negotiations. That vacationing couple was still scowling silently, because coming down here from their room had failed to make them love each other again. Her fellow bartender was still measuring his sideburns in the mirror.

And now there was a new sound, a steady, muffled *clop*, heavy and arrhythmic. Getting closer.

Harmony had a new customer.

He was more unusual with every detail she noticed. Almost eight feet tall. Noble and square face. Broad chest. No clothes. Four legs. Thick brown coat of hair below the waist. Black tail.

Of all the bad jokes Harmony had ever heard, she'd never heard one that starts with a centaur walking into a bar.

But that's what he undeniably was. Hooves instead of toes. Muscles everywhere. Wild and untamed hairdo. He smelled like dark soil that had a thousand things living in it. The Old Spice people would murder children to have the formula for a scent like this.

It took an embarrassingly small amount of time for Harmony to consider the mechanics of fucking the centaur.

The centaur spoke English, but she didn't recognize the drink he was ordering. Her lips and tongue were half-limp: she couldn't stop staring at him. Finally, she apologized, said they didn't carry his request. His eyes flashed displeasure, but he ordered a pitcher of their darkest beer. He grasped it in one giant hand like a regular mug, then strode casually over to the dartboard and made six dart-sized holes in the wall.

She had completely forgotten to ask if he wanted to open a tab. He didn't have anywhere apparent to carry a wallet – oh, wait, there was a tough leather pouch slung across a shoulder by his waist. Runes were carved on it: maybe the centaur word for Burberry.

Harmony's jaw was trying to convince the rest of her head that the floor would be a very nice place to be right now.

A second centaur came in now, and roared in greeting to the first. This one was shorter, wider, more pugnacious in bearing. He bounded across the room to the first, and both reared up and boxed with their front hooves, which then came crack-ing down onto the floor. This play melee resulted in a broken vase, three spilled drinks and a neon sign falling off the wall.

They ordered two more pitchers of beer. Harmony was good enough at her job to recognize members of any species who have decided to stay for a while.

✳❖✳

The next two years of Harmony's life were pure thrill. The centaurs were everywhere; trampling into City Council meetings to speak out against development of green space, recording albums that brought the edge and ambition back to rock and roll, and founding small businesses that brought well-paying manufacturing jobs into urban centers again. Thundering hooves were the answer to housing discrimination in more than one neighborhood. Wall Street was doing tumble-flops: everyone wanted to invest in these booming centaur-owned companies, only none of them went public. Instead, graying assholes in expensive suits wrote best-selling advice books about "The Centaur Method," which contained the same twaddle as their previous advice books, and saw their per-hour consulting rates double.

The cable news channels nattered endlessly, and pleaded with any centaur they could find to come join a thriving round-table discussion with an investment fund manager, the as-yet un-indicted CEO of a bankrupt transnational, and a representative of PETA. But every centaur invited to appear on television did the same thing – gave a haughty, booming laugh, galloped into the nearest bar and started singing songs and breaking windows.

Harmony became expert at making centaur drinks, which were heavy and pungent, and if you weighed less than five hundred pounds a single one would put you under the table for the whole weekend. You'd wake up on Monday morning in a pool of sweat, recalling strange dreams about hunting the Great Boar. These beasts worked hard, and played hard – the revenues at her bar shot up so high they could easily afford the new concrete reinforcements. Trivia night was cancelled indefinitely, and on some nights the sing-a-longs lasted until four.

Good sense came over her and she never bedded one of them, but you heard stories. Doctors and nurses were telling morbid anecdotes about new categories of emergency room visits. Then the female centaurs appeared and all that stopped; instead everyone got distracted by the multitude of challenges to local indecent exposure laws.

Harmony had four songs written in her honor, a record in her town, and her tips skyrocketed. She made a down payment on a house, got a business degree of her own, and partnered with a former parks administrator and a Wiccan priestess to start a centaur events planning firm. The first party was almost too good to be true, and the fire only took an hour or two to extinguish.

Heady with success, she met an earnest and handsome young lawyer from Berkeley who was becoming a superstar in the growing field of centaur law. She ravaged him so thoroughly at night that his marriage proposal came out like a whimpered surrender.

And so, with career and family ahead, it came to be her last night working in the hotel bar. Her regular customers bawled and howled and roared and threw blind punches at anything within reach. She was hoisted to the ceiling, passed from shoulder to shoulder, and was even granted that rarest of honors: she was placed on a centaur's back. The biggest one in the room (by day he made custom-designed iron gates with heart-breaking craftsmanship) carried her around the bar, the lobby, even the hotel courtyard, while they sang of her great feats, none of which she had actually performed but which sounded awe-inspiring. Her cheeks were flushed and her legs tingled, and she couldn't wait to get home and throw her precious fiancée down on the floor.

As the night waned and the crowds dispersed, she was straightening out the glasses on the racks for the last time, wiping out the special centaur mugs with her co-worker's help. And once again she heard that now familiar *clop* sound of a paying customer with four legs.

Only before she turned around, she swore she heard it ordering a club soda. And that didn't make any sense at all. Harmony turned...

And there was a well-groomed centaur, a non-threatening six-foot-something, with a polite smile and little reading glasses, and, tapering up to a relaxed-fit waist, a long, four-legged pair of khakis.

Harmony knew in her heart he wouldn't be the last. And she grieved.

◇◇

TO HOLD THE NOTE

"...Your young and precious eyes are all that I can see
When you're sitting all alone with me."

When Hoyt Mallon heard his own voice on the radio, it was no surprise. It was instead a trip through memory as reflexive as the doctor's little hammer on his knee. He knew the song in every detail – especially the way his younger voice curled over the word "see," as gentle but steady as a watercolor stroke. His younger self laid the long bending note down with a smoothness, he had been told so many times, that had coaxed thousands of young girls down onto picnic blankets and bench seats under thousands of swelling full moons.

Fifty-one years ago, he was a kid just out of high school who sang at dances with his buddies Eldon, Barney, and Vaughn. It didn't matter how dressed up the girls' dates were; Hoyt and his buddies looked so sharp and bright and slick up on stage under the lights, and they were singing, too. So he always met girls. And even if he got socked by someone's boyfriend, it was worth it. Hoyt had never been bothered about punching back. Some nights that was the best part.

After one show, a producer introduced himself. They went to this little studio that recorded hymns by day, mostly. He played a song for them: "All Alone with Me." It was rough, just him singing in his pinched voice over an upright piano, but when the melody got to that "see," Hoyt and his buddies all shuddered a little bit. They could feel the power in it. Hoyt and Barney even arm-wrestled to see who would get to sing lead, and Hoyt won. He wrenched his shoulder so hard to win that it was sore for weeks. Sometimes he could swear he still felt the ache from it.

Two days later, they came into the studio with the full house band set up all around. The producer had even brought in strings like Hoyt had heard on some of the big acts' records. They sang the song through seven times; the last time, just to goof, Hoyt leaned into the microphone right before the instrumental break and slyly breathed, "*Come be alone with me, baby.*"

His buddies slapped their hands over their mouths and doubled over laughing, but when the take was done, the producer's voice, thin and calm, clicked in from the booth. "I think that one's a keeper. Thanks boys."

And over a half-century later, they still played it on the radio, on the oldies stations. Hoyt was also an oldie, lying half-asleep on a lawn chair on his little back patch of grass on a stuffy-hot afternoon, listening to the chatter of the sprinkler and the radio. For two minutes and fourteen seconds, his mind was owned by the memory; he was still able to see the piano player with the pipe in his teeth, and the dainty way the drummer had tapped his brushes to make that beat. He knew the exact smell of the six kinds of tobacco that had hung in that room that day.

The sun flashed out from behind a cloud, and Hoyt felt a twinge in his chest that pushed him into waking and made him sputter, pulling him back from the memory. The phone was ringing, and he took a while to decide if it was worth dragging himself indoors to answer. Not many people called him, and those who did usually demanded money or told him someone had died.

The voice on the other end sounded calm and friendly, old like some voices do. Another small theater in another small town; Hoyt sighed and prepared to decline the invitation. He had no way of getting there, anyway.

But then he heard a word: "engagement." That word made him focus in to remember what word had come just before it. And that word was "open-ended." They didn't want him to cruise into town and cruise back out again. They wanted him headquartered at the theater. Living in town. The featured act. The theater was being renovated, and they were looking for a legend you could put up on a billboard on the highway to draw in travelers; the type of travelers who might stay at a hotel, eat at a restaurant, and whose dollars, may hopes be made real, could even kick off construction of a second theater.

This town had an ambition: not to be the new Branson, but instead the closest you could get in a 200-mile radius. But they needed a marquee seed. Hoyt wondered ruefully if he was nearer the top or the bottom of their "get" list. Their ambition sounded lovely, and the old voice on the phone was as kind as lemonade. But Hoyt had been stiffed by a lot of people who meant well, and something about the mantle of being a town's big draw made him squirm inside. He didn't feel worthy.

There was a vague incredibleness to the whole call; maybe it was that very quality that made it impossible for Hoyt to say anything but that he'd come to town and have a look. When he locked up his house and hefted two suitcases into a neighbor's car for a ride to the bus station, he honestly didn't know when he would be back.

❖

"I'll never be that boy your Daddy wants you to know,
But you whisper my name and I don't want to go..."

Young Hoyt didn't know much about how the record business worked, about deals and labels and distribution. He just knew that he had a record, and he was strutting around telling girls about it the very next day. One girl blushed, looked around from instinct, and then whispered urgently, "Can you get me one? The only thing modern my dad lets us listen to is...*Lawrence Welk!*"

That whisper of hers could have been the biggest thing making a record ever achieved for Hoyt, and it would have satisfied him.

But a DJ in Youngstown ignored what the label men told him to push, and played "All Alone with Me" every hour. Suddenly the label was sending Hoyt money. And people around Youngstown made enough noise that "All Alone with Me" started playing on stations in Cleveland and Pittsburgh. And they were sending Hoyt more money, and putting him and his buddies on buses to sing at shows. He didn't remember how many shows they did, or how many dollars he made, or how many laws they broke.

The women – who's kidding who, they were girls, mostly – trembled in their smart dresses; hair pinned up and soft pink cotton hiding below. It wasn't even a challenge anymore. All he had to do was flutter his eyes in their direction and they fell like pins.

His buddies were jealous; they got plenty of action, but plenty's never enough when someone right next to you is getting more. They made more records, the tours got longer, they started going on TV. So much more money, so many more girls, but no matter how wild it got, it was like he always woke up on that old brown bus, grumbling down the road.

✳✳✳

"What if this dance was our only dance?
What if this chance was our o-only chance?"

Hoyt had a tape of the old songs, and any time he got hired on one of these shows he listened to it on the trip out. He remembered the lyrics well enough. It was a ritual for preparing the show, like tracing a line.

He could practically see the air pushing out of his younger self's lungs when a long note swelled. That insuppressible boyishness he heard, like that full, thick hair he had gooped into a wave so many times back then – the man he was now couldn't re-create it. When it came to his hair, some coloring, careful and ritual combing, and his little wig could together make something that was, while not exactly authentic enough to fool anyone, nonetheless near enough so as not to shock an audience out of the reverie for which they had paid.

It was similar with his voice, to which he paid far more attention than to his remaining follicles. He knew its limits, its notes, its endurance; he knew what whiskey best loosened it up before, and what tea best healed it after. He knew how to limit conversations on performance days. And with a quality suit, bright lights, and a little charm, it was usually good enough, even if the lovely bend on that word "see" just got further and further away from him.

He honestly didn't know if the town (What was its name...*Greeneville*...) intended to provide live musicians, or help him update the aging tapes he used for his solo shows, or even if they wanted him to sing with others. Strange, how he had remembered hearing so much during that phone call, but retained none of the usual details which were, in his touring days, the only ones that mattered from one little town to the next.

❊❊❊

"Being with you is the dream that I miss,
I count every minute until our next kiss."

It lasted three years. Faster than high school. His buddies weren't buddies anymore, they were like dogs cramped up in a cage. They fought on the road, and they could fight on stage just by looking at each other. They could even fight while they were off with girls after the show, just by *hearing* each other. Blacking out was the only way to get a break from a fight, so they got good at it.

And then they would wake up on the bus, and some guy they didn't recognize would be yelling through their headaches that keeping their clothes clean wasn't cheap.

On one night that started out like the others, Hoyt brushed by Vaughn, their long-boned bass singer with the big mouth, in the latest dim and slimy dressing room. Vaughn stuttered awful when he wasn't on stage, but he found his voice just long enough to say, "Just when I thought the stink couldn't get worse." It wasn't the worst thing any of them had said to each other. It wasn't even in the top hundred. But for some reason, they started scrapping right there and it was done. Maybe the way Vaughn said it just got past Hoyt's defenses. Maybe it was because Hoyt had just got off the phone with the woman he'd married two months prior and cheated on eight times already, or maybe it was that Eldon had started bringing a gun everywhere making everything more nervous. Maybe it was because their newest song was a turd and they all knew it, but if they didn't sing it every night for two more months the label would take back any money they hadn't already blown. They kept performing, but when the tour ended, they didn't even need to talk about it. The group was done.

The label put Hoyt out there for another year. He was the star, so he just needed some guys around him, and the label had a talent for digging up good-looking singers. They cut a fat check to the original writer of "All Alone with Me" to see if the magic could be summoned again. But something was gone that wasn't coming back: the sound was changing, the girls had new crushes, who knows what it really was.

Hoyt was twenty-three and he didn't know how to do anything else.

∗∘∗

*"Take my hand, go with me,
Find out how right a night can be"*

The bus passed from the grand interstates down to the state highways threading through trees and farm fields, the concrete narrowing like a channel that would sweep passengers along to Greeneville. It took a day and a stiff night to deliver Hoyt to the little town.

It wasn't comfortable, but most of his life hadn't been comfortable. His taste of luxury had been so brief, and yet he had been so ungrateful. How long had it taken him to feel entitled to it – weeks? How long after it was gone did he think it was bound to come back soon? Years.

Somehow he'd managed to live himself a life. He lost money in the divorce. He had less to lose in the second divorce but lost more anyway, because the two of them had a son. He did a turn in the Army, and made it back from that alive. He heard Barney didn't.

He got into selling outdoor pools, which a lot of the young families in the suburbs coveted. The wives would recognize him, sometimes. A little mischief even came of it, but the fights weren't as fun as they used to be.

Checks still came from the records, but they weren't too big, and got smaller after the lawyers sliced them up. He saw his son sometimes and they never really clicked, though Hoyt liked to think they took an honest shot at it. He drank more than his share, and made it back from that alive. He heard Eldon didn't.

At some point, it started to pick up again. He had lived long enough for nostalgia to find him. He appeared in commercials for record collections that had "All Alone with Me" on them. The song showed up in a couple of movies, and the checks got a little bigger. Then a promoter got him and Vaughn back together. Vaughn had opened a hardware store, and they hadn't talked for twenty-five years. Looking at the middle-aged man who used to be his fiercest friend, bent a little at the back, gray, it was like Hoyt wanted to fight him all over again, but just didn't have the energy. Vaughn seemed to feel the same way, and they never talked about it.

They got paired up with two other middle-aged guys whose groups had fallen apart. The promoter had a talent for digging up guys like that. With new suits and a little hair dye, they could put on a fair show, and they only needed to do a few songs. Truth be told, the audience probably only needed one.

They toured like that for a couple of years. Hoyt kept better track of his money, didn't drink. On the bus he read books and drank tea or napped across the countryside.

A hotel in Laughlin booked them for four months, and that felt great. They had their act polished, and the promoter sprang for a doctor that smoothed a few lines out of Hoyt's face. Vaughn declined the offer. "They ain't seeing me," he said.

The promoter hoped the hotel would extend the contract. It didn't. He thought the group would get picked up somewhere else. It didn't. Hoyt spent three months living in the cheapest apartment he could find in Nevada, waiting to hear news. The days were too long and too bright; it seemed like all he did from wake to sleep was sweat. He felt the itch to drink all the time. He tried to pass the time with hired girls instead; they were friendly, but it was expensive company.

One day as the summer was finally loosening its grip, Vaughn knocked at his door. He said he missed his store and his family and he was going home. As they shook hands, the feeling that this was the last time they would see each other washed over Hoyt, and he felt he should say something. All he had was, "You remember that night when I walked in on you losing your cherry?"

Vaughn crinkled his eyes and smiled. "I think when I saw you I made a sound like...buh hu-buh hu-buh hu-buh."

They shared a laugh, and that was all.

❊❖❊

"Others may promise to cherish you too,

But I am the one who will always be true"

Another twenty years drifted by, and life never got a lot better, but there were times Hoyt could see it had gotten a little better. He sold some more pools and found a third wife who stayed with him for eight full years and wasn't even all that mad at him when she left. He lost nothing in that divorce. Most years he could piece together a decent living off the old checks and odd gigs.

His body sagged and his hair retreated to the back of his head. He bought a little wig he put on for those occasions when someone hired him to put on a show. He drove himself to the gigs now, had his own tape to sing in front of, because most of the time you couldn't trust the locals to put a decent band together. He treated these jobs like small getaways, paid for with a song.

There was a sameness to the towns that had made the younger Hoyt contemptuous. But the things that were the same had a way of comforting him now, and he had a better eye for the little things that were different. And so shows would go south, club owners would try to rip him off, all the frustrations and indignities you might guess happened, but as much as he might blow his stack on the spot, enough miles down the road and it didn't seem to matter anymore. There was always another town.

At 230,000 miles his car finally gave up the ghost, and when that happened Hoyt looked around at his life and started to think he might just stop running after money. He didn't have much put away, but he felt bone-tired and soul-weary.

He hadn't gathered many friends, and he didn't fish or golf. Things got dark for him as he thought about the nearness of death. He'd never been much for church except as a place to sing, but he had vague worries that he hadn't fed the hungry enough or things like that. He thought about the number of things he'd done that could have seen him tossed in jail if someone with a broken jaw had pressed charges, or if one too-young girl had turned out to be the daughter of the local sheriff.

Is this the span of my life? Hoyt wondered on many nights. *Am I on my last curve down?*

⁕⁕⁕

So this was Greeneville. Hoyt had made a game of guessing the population of a town by the size and upkeep of its downtown. For Greeneville, he guessed 3,000 at most; its small helping of two-story brick buildings didn't extend far from the town square with its humble war monument. But he had sung in smaller burgs, both in the earliest days and the latest ones.

He met local business leaders, the owner of the theater, the mayor. This was an unusual honor, but it was an unusual investment they were proposing to make in him. They smiled and greeted him with happiness and humility, sharing their admiration, the memories that his songs had laced in their lives. Had he played this Greeneville before?

They set him up in a small apartment over the drug store, right across the street from the theater. They escorted him through the theater, where even as they walked its wide aisles, local sons were beating dust off chairs and scrubbing through years of old grime. As Hoyt walked by, one picked up a campaign button for a forgotten congressional hopeful from 1970.

The days before opening flowed into each other. He shook more hands. The owner of the AA baseball team asked him to sing the national anthem and "Take Me Out to the Ballgame" during games, and though Hoyt didn't see much recompense from that but free seats, hot dogs, and beer, it felt fair and the folks on the wooden bleachers were some of the warmest and most appreciative he could remember.

At night he looked down into the quiet street and wrangled with his restlessness. What was happening? Nothing. Why this particular breed of nothing? Hoyt stared for hours out the window and couldn't answer. But soon, there would be a show to do, and that was enough.

There was no back-up band, and no back-up singers. Just Hoyt and his old tape. The night of the opening, he treated his apartment as his dressing room, and with his makeup and brushes and pins and wig he assembled the him people would pay to see. His suit – a rich burgundy that caught the light well – came out of a fresh dry-cleaning bag, but it held an old smell that he and no one else would always be able to detect.

He didn't know quite what to expect when he emerged from his stairwell onto the street. What he saw was a small collection of citizens under the light of the marquee, acknowledging him with glances and smiles, but keeping their distance. No talk of autographs. No pleading eyes.

With only a small hesitation, Hoyt crossed the street and walked through the front doors. A young stagehand guided him to the dressing room, which smelled damp. A bouquet of flowers brightened it, as did a gift basket containing handmade candles that were the famed specialty of one of the local women. Sitting on top of the basket was a deeply apologetic note asking Hoyt to not use the candles in the theater, because of the risks.

Back in his prime, this would be the hour to sneak in as much drink or reefer and private time in dark spaces with dazzled women as could be managed before the label man forced all of them onto the stage. Now there seemed no more sense to those urges than there was in denying the truth of the painted old man reflected in the big mirror. Hoyt settled himself on the couch – a battered veteran, too short for his legs – and dozed until the knock at his door.

Hoyt had taken tens of thousands of steps onto thousands of stages, and had arrived to nearly every response between ecstasy, ambivalence, and hostility. He had shut much of himself off from caring. But on this night he felt the weight of his steps more, and could only blame the ambition the town had invested in him. He wanted this audience to be happy to see him. He wished he could scan every silhouette and ask, *are you a local or a visitor? Did I bring you here from far away?*

He could read nothing from the figures in the half-filled chairs but kind attention. His ears caught the subtle click and hiss of his tape, and with perfect timing his foot stepped out on the first drum beat – not a dance move, but a means to open himself up for the kind of rhythmic swaying that would pass for a dance from his old joints for the course of the evening. He grinned wide. "Good evening, Greeneville!" he sang into the microphone, and heard a ripple of claps and whistles wishing him the same.

This was what Hoyt knew – that his job was to make that which was real outside the theater shimmer out of being for the audience, and instead navigate them through currents of memory and feeling, the young hopes that outlasted their youth and carried them through hard times, and the sweet sadnesses that could not be described with a color or a face. These songs weren't food, they weren't a roof against the rain, and they didn't raise the dead nor make an empty bed full. But they did something people were grateful for, and Hoyt called it the greatest lesson in his life that, when the girls in the crowd stopped screaming, he'd kept singing long enough to learn it.

He talked about the old times between songs – not his own experiences, but the time that they had all passed through together. This had become part of his show when he had reached the point of needing a breather, and the crowd listened and chuckled and clapped.

He closed, as he always did now, with a special version of "All Alone with Me": one that started with a long instrumental, over which he would tell just a bite of the story of the four stupid kids who wanted to be big shots at the dance. The first verse would follow, slower than on the record, and Hoyt would close his eyes and tilt his head up into his best light. It was a gesture that he knew made him look like he was transporting himself back through his mind, and it beckoned the audience to follow. For a long time he just struck the pose, but in his later years it seemed like courtesy to really go through with it, and think of those days as he sang.

When the song hit its right tempo, he put in every last ember he had for it, swaying, clapping and stepping with a giant smile. On the good nights, the crowd would stand up and dance. This made itself one of those nights.

The lights dropped, and the applause pounded the walls of the old theater. Hoyt felt it bathe him, feed him, revive him. And when the lights came up, and the reprise of the song played, for the first time in many, many years, he nearly forgot to take his bow.

He paused in his dressing room, after he had toweled off the sweat and changed into simple street clothes, to listen to the theater – its ancient creaks, the vibrations of its walls. It had been an instrument in the ovation, cupping and carrying the applause through its rafters and dusty hollows. It had a voice; every theater did, and since he would be here for a little while now, he wished to know it as a partner. And – if he knew how – to honor it.

Hoyt once again used the main theater doors rather than the stage door. Many of the older patrons were still happily clotted together talking about the entertainment, with ones and twos breaking away for a slow walk home under the stars. You could see so many stars in Greeneville.

This was the first of many good shows. Some tourists did come, and mingled with the Greeneville crowd. Hoyt couldn't figure why the locals came to see his show repeatedly. He wondered if arrangements were made at the box office to give him a full and friendly crowd for the sake of the visitors: if everyone was just pulling their weight to make this a success. Hoyt tried his best, within his scripted show, taped music, and weary muscles, to make it lively for them all, for the new ones that they might tell their friends, and the others from sheer gratitude. It spurred him to entertain until he ached.

He established friendly rounds in Greeneville: a diner with plain coffee; a barbershop that would discretely draw the shades and work with him privately; a divorcee in her 40's – Bless it, her hot 40's! – who invited him around to her place once in a while. The radio station gave him a show where he would dedicate songs to lovers. Greeneville wasn't a big town, but it seemed to have a lot of lovers.

The snow fell and then melted away. The theater wasn't getting any cleaner, and there were no new acts following. Just Hoyt and his old tape. He had a little money, and he wondered if he ought to try and get a new tape made, to spruce up the show. But the local school needed basketball uniforms, and acting on an urge he had never felt before, he found himself becoming a donor.

At some point, there just weren't strange faces in the crowd anymore. The tourists had moved on, or more likely just forgot Greeneville was there. A small bug of anxiousness crawled inside him, that this marked the march to the inevitable, and he would soon be fired. He didn't feel like he'd failed; it was just a thing that hadn't worked, like so many things have time to not work in life.

He kept to his business. Cleaned his suit before every show. Sang and remembered. Heard the applause from the half-full and falling-apart chairs. Were any of them even paying any more? How did the math work? When he was young, Hoyt hadn't cared as long as he got his. Now he got his without fail, and suddenly their selfless generosity made him feel like he owned every light meal and unmended window in Greeneville.

One Monday, with three days to himself, he got a notion to take a drive. He hadn't left Greeneville for a year. He still liked everything about it, he just suddenly wanted to take a drive. So he packed a small bag and left behind the hairpiece and the suit and the tape. He got in the old car the dentist had sold him, and rolled along Main Street until the buildings were behind and the road became the highway.

He didn't remember how far away the next town would be, and for awhile it was just a barn here or there, and the most amazing quiet. He flipped on the radio and turned it to Greeneville's station, where they were playing a recording of one of his shows. It was his own voice, but only a few dozen miles away, it was already fading out. He switched it off just as he saw the signs of another town ahead.

It had a small main street, like Greeneville. A good place for a look around and a simple lunch. Hoyt parked and stepped out and looked around. But the place was empty. Every store was closed, and there wasn't a dogwalker nor a local son on the streets.

It wasn't a holiday. Hoyt peered in some windows, and now saw clues of decay in the weeds and dust insinuating itself everywhere. The town was abandoned; this was an unusual thing, but the kind of thing you heard about. Times were bad. So he stretched his rickety limbs and returned to the car and his drive.

It was in that amazing quiet of the road that Hoyt realized he had not seen another car for hours. He had maybe not seen or even heard another car since Greeneville. This was beyond unusual, and he flipped on the radio, suddenly wanting another voice.

But every station played static. AM, FM, they didn't have any melodies for him.

He saw the outlines of another town on the horizon, and he pressed the gas, speeding towards it. The only thing that kept his apprehension short of outright fear was that he couldn't even name what it was he feared.

This town was small like the last one, and like Greeneville, humble and with history. But it too was empty – every person gone, no sign of what had happened. And nature, in its patient way, was retaking the place for the soil.

Hoyt could have gone on: looked for the interstate, found a phone and called an old friend or even a random stranger just to see, just to know this emptiness wasn't everywhere. But instead, his hands ahead of his will, he turned the wheel and pointed the car back, towards Greeneville.

118

It was a long drive, and the sun started to set. He kept the radio tuned, and as night took hold he found his own voice, recorded at the station, playing everyone's requests.

Hoyt remembered the show, and knew what songs would be coming up, including that inevitable time when he would put on his own.

Greeneville was still there. He still had a gig. The moon lit the heartland and he turned up the radio and listened to those old words that he had nailed on take seven back in that studio when he was barely a man.

"…Your young and precious eyes are all that I can see
When you're sitting all alone with me."

◇◇*

EVAN AFTER HE GOT FIRED

DAY ONE

Evan didn't know what time it was exactly when he stopped sleeping. He wasn't ready to commit to opening his eyes. Some dream was dissolving about a tree the size of a skyscraper with roots that curled around mountains. When it passed he finally squinted his eyes open, and saw the shape of his girlfriend Adriane wrapped in the sheet next to him.

He rolled onto his back and considered the ceiling. How many nights had it been over his head since he moved into this apartment? A thousand? Almost a thousand. Strange how little he thought about it.

Adriane dropped an arm across his chest and looked up into his eyes. Her morning breath brushed his nostrils, and he ignored it as he always did. That was the same. Many things were exactly the same as they had been yesterday. "Stay right there," she whispered. "Stay right there." Then she rose, stretched, and made that little squeak noise that always made Evan smile. She slid into his robe and padded out of the bedroom.

What a girlfriend Adriane was. Last night, after he had called with the news, she had rushed over with a weekend bag and taken him out to dinner at a restaurant he loved. She didn't probe about his plans, just held his hand and listened as he talked about his unexpected last day at work. Then, back at his place, she treated him to a long backrub and a medium-length blowjob; the kind where she gives you a clear sign that it isn't meant for foreplay but just to lie back and have. What a girlfriend she was.

Evan stared at the wall. It was a dreary near-white. Maybe he could paint it. He wasn't sure if he was allowed; he'd have to check with the landlord. He worriedly considered that there were a thousand simple questions about his life he had just never asked.

Adriane re-entered, carrying a tray of breakfast. "Eggs," she purred. "Eggs will make you feel strong." There was bacon, too, and as he ate, she cuddled next to him, stealing little bits of it.

"You're still pampering me?" He looked at her, feeling blessed beyond the experience of mortals.

"All day," she whispered, kissing his shoulder. "And all night too." And she kissed it again.

Evan did feel strength coming on, like lightning surging into his arms. With the eggs and her love, he could lift a car like a superhero. He looked at her and laughed at the thought of it; she picked up the laughter and added her own.

She made good on her promise all day. They went to the park for a long walk, and he marveled at the simple good of fresh air, and sunshine, and not looking at one's watch. Adriane proposed that they buy bicycles in the near future, and Evan loved this idea. They wiled away happy hour with fried food and beer, and then back at the apartment she sat with patient revulsion through one of the gruesome horror movies that made Evan whoop and cackle. This was truly a more giving gesture than the previous night's oral.

They shared some weed in a long bath, then settled down with a good cozy screw. As she passed into contented sleep, Evan stared back up at that ceiling. His brain turned over all the pleasures of the day, meditating on how cinched up his life had become in his work that he hadn't stopped to enjoy it in so long.

He could take this chance to change that. He would get another job, but this time he would keep his perspective. This was about more than a paycheck: this was about living better, and it was all possible.

Others fell apart when these challenges hit them. Evan would not fall apart.

He thought about it for a long time before he slept. He felt strong.

DAY TWO

Again Evan didn't know what time it was when he woke; again it was not important. Still in his pajamas, his hair absolutely not giving a damn about itself, he joined Adriane for breakfast. She had to go to her office, which she often did Sundays before a work trip. She looked so polished and professional and he complimented her on it. He vowed to never let a day go by without saying something nice to her. She deserved that.

Sunday was not the day for job hunting, but this revival inside him did not want to wait. He surveyed his apartment with new authority. Those shelves could be better organized. Everything (God, EVERYTHING) could be dusted. He started with laundry – tomorrow he would look for work, and dressing like a professional would put the right vibe out into the universe.

During the long phone call with his parents, as they quizzed him on his plans and said over and over what a good, hard-working boy he was, his hand fell on his old exercise bike, long ago repurposed as a rack for un-ironed clothes. With a swell of wild ambition he cleared the clothing away. He gave the pedals a test spin, and felt a thrum inside him, as if he were grazing the edge of a great power.

Finally he made an excuse, said good-bye to his parents, and changed into old sweat pants. He put on music – music with loud guitars, played loudly. He pedaled himself into a glorious sweat, and didn't stop until his legs throbbed.

After a shower, the quiet of the apartment made him restless. Inspiration told him to cook dinner for Adriane. He hardly ever cooked, and this would both give his girlfriend something to enjoy and contribute to the general equality of modern times.

Evan searched the Internet and settled on the first recipe that included the words "chicken" and "pasta." He went giddy at the supermarket picking out fresh vegetables; then, back at the apartment, delivered himself over to the alien world of mixing and measuring, sipping a couple of beers along the way.

By the time Adriane got home, he had set the table so goddamn nice. Adriane was delighted, and insisted on uncorking a bottle of wine. Over dinner, they talked about the trip she would be on for the next week, but soon they just fell silent and gazed at each other, enlivened by the way they were answering this test from life.

In bed, his brain tumbled from all the alcohol. It would be fine; it was a celebration, a salute to the beginning of a new chapter. On a sudden whim he sat up and looked out his bedroom blinds, and swore he saw the streaking end of a shooting star.

DAY THREE

Evan's legs were in agony. He had felt the ache growing during the night, but dismissed it. Now, stiff and peevish, his over-biked legs snarled against getting out of bed. Adriane playfully dragged him out. They breakfasted and then she left with a kiss, off to her home and then the airport for her work trip.

It was time. It was Monday.

Evan took coffee. And aspirin. He soaked in the tub for his sore muscles, then shaved, dressed up, and sat down at the computer.

He visited the major classified sites, sorted the real prospects from the ridiculous, and within an hour had sent out five resumes. The action of copying and pasting the query letter had such a satisfying rhythm. Evan felt like he could write a book about how to navigate these moments. Maybe he and Adriane could write it together. And then the riches would shower down and he wouldn't even need a new job. She could quit hers and then they could go on motivational tours together and make love in fancy hotels.

He took a break and watched some porn. A man needed his means to survive the time apart.

After lunch he relaxed. He had been more productive in this half day off than he had been in many full days at his old job. His legs were too sore for a walk, but he sat out on his small balcony, sipped a beer, and enjoyed the afternoon light. The sound of kids playing in the street drifted up to him. This idleness was so valuable; he could feel the thoughts and worries of the day folding themselves away in the drawers of his brain. He decided to extend it by the length of another beer.

DAY FOUR

Evan felt thick. His face was sunburned and his stomach made angry gurgles. Dinner had happened very late the night before; a fast food meal, not good to sleep on. He tugged himself from the bed and over to the computer to watch some porn.

It was already 10:00. Phone calls were the mission for the day. He remembered assigning himself that. Calling at 10:00 was too early; it made him look eager, and Evan wasn't so eager that he would work just anywhere. He wanted the universe to know that. *Evan is not unemployed. Evan is free to choose where he will work.* That was his mantra.

His legs felt recovered enough for a walk, so he headed for a café he had passed many times. On other days he might have used the car, but this was better, healthier.

He ordered something flamboyant from a girl with bright orange hair. She was bent over the countertop, scribbling in a little book. After Evan stole a look at her body he was struck by the impulse to appear involved with something, anything. He fished for his phone and lobbed greetings to a few acquaintances. Even this could be counted as productive. Who knew who in his circle might have a lead on his next job?

He saw an e-mail from Adriane: *Hope all's well! :).* The brevity of it seemed slightly patronizing. He shoved the phone back in his pocket and turned his attention to his drink.

"Oh wait," said the girl with the orange hair. "I forgot the topper; do you mind if I put it on?" She answered his blank face by taking the initiative to sprinkle a secret mixture onto the foam of his drink. She smiled. "This is what makes it, right here."

Evan marveled as she turned back to her little book. He sipped, and she was so utterly right. It made the drink. It made his morning. He all but jogged home so he could masturbate to her image as soon as possible.

It was just past noon after he finished. No reason to call anyone just after noon, really, not during lunch. In fact, since some professionals took lunch at noon and some at one, it wasn't savvy to try anyone at all until two. So he pulled a box of DVDs off the shelf – that show Adriane was always telling him he would love. He would watch it, and then he would send her a message telling her how much he loved it, and that would be the nice thing he said to her that day.

He felt so efficient. He popped in the DVD and settled on the couch. After one episode there was time for a second, and after the second there was still time for at least part of a third before two p.m.

At four, he panicked. Sheer inertia had carried him through two discs' full of shows, and now the business day was winding down. He made it off the couch and halfway to his desk where he had left his list of phone numbers to call. But then he stopped. Calling in an agitated mood would make him seem desperate, not to mention a procrastinator for inquiring so late. Better to take it easy, sleep well, give the task his best at the most opportune moment tomorrow.

He embraced this wisdom, calmed himself, popped open a beer, and put in another disc of the show. Everything would still be where it needed to be in the morning.

DAY FIVE

When Evan got out of bed, his arm fell off. He didn't notice at first – he was a side sleeper, so he was used to his arm going dead in the night, then tingling and fuzzing its way back to life.

He stood, still dazed, remembering how the characters from that TV show had occupied his dreams, taking him along on their adventures like a good luck mascot. He thought about how he was starving because he had skipped dinner, and how he really wanted the biggest pancake ever created, but he also liked the idea of another of the orange-haired girl's coffee specials. He stumbled through the bathroom doorway, which normally would have bumped his right arm against the frame.

Only nothing bumped, not even audibly. This slowly dawned on Evan as strange. He reached to feel his arm, only the arm wasn't actually there. He looked down to where it was supposed to be, even turned a circle like a dog chasing its tail. It wasn't there. His shoulder just...ended, at a smooth round nub. No cut, no scar, just skin covering bone.

The words *Call somebody!* screamed through his mind.

His phone was on the table by the bed. And there he saw his arm, still shoved under the hypoallergenic pillow he had bought for Adriane but which he often stole in the night because, deep down, he liked it better than all the others.

He picked up the arm. Was it heavier than he expected an arm to be? Lighter? He had no expectations to confound; he had just never wondered. It was still warm. He shook it, and it flopped. He felt no sensation from touching it, even when he pinched the flesh. He turned it over, fascinated, seeing it from angles he had never before considered.

"CALL SOMEBODY!" Those were still the only words his mind could cook up from the primordial soup of panic and confusion bubbling in his subconscious behind his paused face.

He pushed the top end of the arm against his shoulder nub and held it there. Maybe it would just re-attach. He was still close enough to his dreams to think it possible he was in a world that worked this way.

It did not.

He let go of the arm and gravity took it to the floor. He winced when he saw the fingers splay in funny ways on landing.

He sent a text to Adriane: *My arm fell off! What do I do?* This took a really long time with only one arm. Moments later, she answered: *Stopping jerking off, silly! Didn't your Mother ever warn you this would happen? :P*

It was his masturbating arm.

Evan grabbed his car keys. And duct tape.

⋄⋄*

At the emergency room check-in, it was a dumb joke on Evan that he had to write, with his left hand, that his problem was that his right arm had fallen off. He was not left-handed, and the words looked like they'd been written by a palsied four-year old.

He felt conspicuous holding his arm in his lap, sticky residue still on the end from his failed attempt to tape it back to his shoulder. If it were a baby or a pet, he would have it wrapped in a blanket; that sounded right, and yet he couldn't be sure the same etiquette applied to limbs.

Time passed. He checked his e-mail on his phone regularly, hoping to receive some reply from a job query that he could review ten or fifteen times to pass the hours. All around him were sad, worried people sneezing or bleeding or who knew what else. Not a single one had any reaction to the young man sitting by the candy machine holding a naked arm.

⋄⋄*

The doctor struck a jovial tone. "Nothing else falling off, I hope?"

Evan laughed a little in a worried attempt to treat this as normally as everyone else was. He handed over his arm. "This isn't enough?"

The doctor examined the fingers for broken bones, then turned the arm over and checked the wrist for a pulse. Whatever he felt there (Evan wasn't placing bets), it pleased him. "Oh, I'm sure it's an inconvenience, but it's nothing unusual."

"I...I've never heard of this. I mean ever."

"Well, it would be a pretty boring world if it were only full of things you've heard of."

Evan was struck by the truth of that, but persisted. "It's really freaky. I mean, I didn't feel it happen."

"Well, I could give you the medical explanation. It's about resonant fields of life energy, and there's a lot of Latin words. But basically, your arm doesn't want to be connected to you right now."

"Doesn't...what?"

The doctor looked at an old poster on the wall, as if already thinking ahead to future patients. "I don't think I can boil it down any more than that, son. Your arm doesn't want to be attached. Now, I could slice it open, slice open your shoulder, call in a team to do twelve hours of surgery on your nerves and blood vessels, force the whole thing together and hope you don't die, but I don't recommend that."

Awed, Evan asked a question he had managed not to ask for five days.

"What do I do?"

"I can give you pills. Won't get your arm to cooperate again, but it'll help with the freaking out part. Are you insured?"

Evan was recently unemployed. "I don't know?"

"You ought to make your statements sound like statements and your questions like questions. That's not medical advice, I'm just trying to be generally helpful."

"What do I do about my arm?"

"Anything recent happen in your life that your arm might not be happy about?"

"I...well I left my job."

"There you go. Always a major life change there. Probably just some issues with that."

"Is this, like, something I should see a therapist about?"

The doctor rummaged in his pocket and found a business card. "I don't think therapy gets you too far in these situations. Voodoo's good, though. I can recommend a good Voodoo guy."

DAY SIX

Evan barely slept that night: his mind kept spinning helplessly round and round about where to put the arm. If it decided to reattach itself in the night, he didn't want it stuck in the sock drawer. Would it crawl to him on its own? Every mental avenue led somewhere creepy. But if he kept it in the bed, he risked rolling over it in the night. That sounded damaging.

Ultimately, he'd placed it on the nightstand, which meant he had to find alternate places for his magazine pile, ashtray, Playstation Portable, receipts, and some empty beer bottles.

On the plus side, he wasn't hungover this morning. He did, however, feel the strong urge to find a breakfast already prepared for him, and that he could eat with one hand.

He stuck his arm in a backpack and walked to the café.

The orange-haired girl wore a nametag – it said "Carl." Evan guessed this was irony. He asked for the same beverage as before, and treasured the little sprinkle she added at the end. He tried to pivot it into a conversation. "So, when did you discover that?"

Girl-Carl was already opening her little book. "What?"

"That little mixture you put on. You said it's what makes it."

She stuffed a bookmark into the book and looked at him with alarm. "Okay, this is weird. I didn't talk to you at all."

"No. No, you said it to me last time I was here."

"Oh! Jeez, you got me worried; I was wondering if I was, like, projecting my thoughts. I wouldn't want that happening. A lot of my thoughts are private, you know?"

Evan hadn't known where he wanted the conversation to go when he started it, but he didn't imagine it getting here. It was like getting two moves into a chess game and your opponent starts drawing on the squares with a glitter pen.

"Have you ever seen anything like this?" he asked, pulling the arm out of the backpack.

Girl-Carl immediately screamed. He was so relieved.

"I know – it's weird, right? I haven't known what to do with it since it fell off."

She was still fanning her face violently with both hands, murmuring some weak mantra to herself. Then those words sunk in. "It's yours?"

"Yeah." He wiggled his empty shoulder.

Girl-Carl made a massive exhalation, her voice starting at a high pitch and traveling down two octaves as the air escaped. And suddenly she was completely soothed. "Oh my GOD. I don't know why I didn't think of that. I just saw that and thought you had, like, chopped off somebody else's arm."

"Why would I show that to you? Wait...are you saying the fact that it's my own arm makes it not scary anymore?"

"Well, sure. I mean I've never seen it before but I could see that happening. Can I see it again?"

Suddenly her book was forgotten and Evan's coffee was going cold. He produced the arm again. She grinned. "Roll up your other sleeve!" She bounced between looking at the two. "Hold them next to each other! They totally belong to each other! You can tell. That could be a game: 'Do These Arms Belong on the Same Person?' I would rock that game."

Evan felt his forehead cooking. Then she asked, "Can I touch it?"

He said "Sure!" very quickly.

◦

Girl-Carl said that she was going to see her friend's awesome band that evening, and that it would change Evan's life if he went and heard them. His plan had been to register with a temp agency, but he realized his current condition would sabotage his typing speed. Instead he went to a second-hand store, hoping to find something cool to wear.

He scratched under his chin as he scanned the racks. He hadn't shaved in a couple of days, but maybe it didn't matter. He would shave as soon as he had an interview. A little stubble could be cool. Tonight, he could be a guy with stubble seeing a local band.

His phone buzzed with a voicemail from Adriane, the words made intermittent by some faraway outdoor breeze. *Sorry I missed you, just wanted to...flight changed, I'll send you...hope you're dominating out there! Many many kisses!*

A phone call to say she would be emailing him. A pulse of irritation worked through Evan head to toe.

* ❊❖❊ *

Evan found the bar where the band was playing. After spending the first set pressed against a slightly slimy wall, he spied girl-Carl and pushed his way towards her like a slow train through cattle. She was giddy and sweaty, and the band wasn't so great, but two hours, seven drinks, and fifteen songs about starry nights and mean girls later, he found himself in a car that might have been hers, where she gave him a handjob with the same dainty joy with which she made coffee beverages, while his connected arm plunged hungrily down her shirt.

DAY SEVEN

Evan had no idea what time it was when he finally let the light in. His head felt like a puddle of mud with horses stomping through it. His traumatized eardrums refused to believe in the quiet. His memory was a melting swirl – smells like ashtrays and hairspray, sounds of breathing and a groaning car seat, a dream where his parents sprouted fifty heads each to yell at him, the delicious foreign texture of a breast not belonging to his longtime girlfriend.

An email. Adriane was going to email him about her flight. Evan rolled over to pick up his phone.

His remaining arm did not obey. His remaining arm was no longer remaining. So nothing stopped Evan as he fell out of bed.

Lying on the floor, suffering, Evan noticed that he was wearing only last night's briefs. Questions unfurled themselves in the light, slowly, like flowers. How had he undressed himself? How had he even entered his apartment? Most vitally of all – *where was his other arm?*

The right arm still sat in his backpack, which now rested on top of his dresser. The other was nowhere in sight. He checked under the bed: no arm. With great dexterity, he managed to pull open his dresser drawers using his toes. No arm.

It was time to vomit.

With the toilet lid down, Evan made the emergency decision to heave into the bathtub. He then used his feet to turn on the water and switch the flow up to the shower head, which he used to wash out his mouth along with the tub. Then he just let his head rest under the spray.

What day was it? When he was employed, he could always at least narrow it down by the days left until the weekend. Friday. It was Friday. Only a week since he had lost his job. No leads yet. Not too big a concern, because he would be collecting unemployment...

He'd forgotten to fill out the unemployment paperwork. And now he had no arms. He groaned under the running water.

To an outside observer, it would have seemed like Evan spent the next twenty minutes staring dully at his phone. What was going on inside though, which lacked anything near the available energy to express itself physically, was a slow fever. With all the strategy he could tug out of the swamp in his head, he was trying to navigate the multi-dimensional bugfuck nightmare that had become his life between last night and then. And he was running into the same stupid dead ends over and over like a lab rat after too many paint fume tests.

So many answers involved calling someone. Normally he would call Adriane, but he didn't know if she was still gone, in the air, or already here and wondering where he was. And he couldn't go to get her, because he couldn't drive. In fact, he couldn't leave his apartment alone, because he wouldn't be able to lock it behind him. His wasn't the best neighborhood, but it had been all he could afford because he hadn't shown much ambition at work, probably because once he had started receiving sexual attention from a hot non-insane woman on a regular basis he lost whatever motivation he ever had for trying to be impressive, and he had also....

Cheated on her.

He would come upon that thought sometimes, and it always struck quietly but firmly, like the thump of a low, distant kettle drum. To the best of his knowledge there had been no actual sex last night, and based on that, Evan decided the chivalrous thing would be to just not mention it. It had been meaningless, he was clearly not in his right mind, and that girl had practically dragged him into it.

This was just a momentary setback. He had deviated from the path so gradually that he hadn't noticed, but now, reflecting in the unforgiving light of the morning after, Evan saw where he had squandered his early momentum.

His head started to clear. It was time to put those things behind him. Time to put the booze away...not like he could do much drinking with no arms anyway, right? He chuckled at this thought, pushing the throat phlegm around.

Time to refocus on finding a job. That would set things right. He could check his emails on his computer, surf using his foot on the mouse. Evan felt confidence returning. *Others must go through this*, he thought, and here he was, more aware, ahead of the curve.

And then he saw the card his doctor had given him – the Voodoo guy.

Time to face the problem head on. Expense be damned. He'd functioned for days with one arm. With two arms restored, he would be unstoppable.

He dialed using his nose. The Voodoo man, who called himself Mr. Juge, promised to make a house call in an hour, and asked if Evan was allergic to cats. Evan was not.

He managed to dress using his toes, his mouth, and the wall to slide a shirt down his torso. He checked his email: Adriane would be landing in two hours. As long as Mr. Juge could work his spell before then, Evan could make it.

He unlocked the door, so when the soft knock came, he simply announced "Come on in!" in a voice that tried to suggest devil-may-care relaxation. He sat in a cross-legged pose on the couch.

Mr. Juge certainly didn't look like a Voodoo priest. He wore a simple, slick black suit; in one hand was a satchel, in the other a pet carrier. He didn't say hello, but simply stated, in a luscious voice, "You are the afflicted one." Evan nodded. Mr. Juge set down his things and, making little "puss puss puss" sounds, opened the pet carrier.

A black cat emerged and considered its surroundings, making an occasional noise as if commenting on the spaciousness, or to express pity about the state of the walls. "Do not disturb it," Mr. Juge said sternly.

Evan was still trying to figure out how to participate in the conversation. Finally he managed a simple question. "So you do Voodoo?"

"Strange question, sir. Do you do seeing and hearing?"

"I just meant, you don't...well you don't look..."

Mr. Juge swiftly pulled a wrapped bundle of greasy bristles from his satchel and whacked it across Evan's face. While Evan recovered from the surprise, Mr. Juge pulled a large gold hoop from his pocket and clipped it inside his nose. "This is more what you are expecting?"

Evan nodded sheepishly. The black cat was diligently carving trails in the arm of his couch.

Now Mr. Juge reached back in the satchel and produced a small stuffed character Evan recognized from a Japanese cartoon. He encouraged Evan to lie back on the couch and then placed the character on his chest, facing him. "That is your *gris-gris*. Your good luck."

"It looks like something you buy at a gas station."

"That is where I bought it. Where the *gris-gris* comes from is irrelevant."

"What do I do with it?"

"Consider it."

Evan looked at it, and wondered if this constituted considering it. "What do I consider about it?"

"Consider if you can believe it will bring you luck. Consider it until you can or you quit. I am now going to use your stove. Where do you keep your saucepans?"

While Evan stared at the stuffed animal, Mr. Juge stirred and pinched and made stinking smoke over at the stove. At one point he squeezed some honey from a little bear bottle Evan had forgotten he owned.

The black cat jumped onto the couch, pushed the *gris-gris* off onto the floor, and started kneading at Evan's chest, claws included. Evan cringed and started to sit up, but Mr. Juge barked, "Do NOT disturb it!" So Evan stayed still while the cat scraped through his shirt again and again before curling into a little fur disc there.

"My *gris-gris* is on the floor," Evan complained.

"You complain too much," replied Mr. Juge. He pulled a child's sippy cup from his satchel, and filled it with murky liquid from the saucepan. Referring to the cup, he said, "Knowing your condition, I brought this. Please do not read any subtext into it whatsoever."

Suddenly an image blasted itself, widescreen, into Evan's mind. He saw his other arm. He saw it on the floor of a car, under a plain black zip-up hoodie next to crumpled fast food bags, a pair of sneakers, postcards for club parties that had ended over a year ago, and a dozen home-burned CDs labeled with magic marker.

Of course it had fallen off in girl-Carl's car. Perhaps she had brought him home.

Mr. Juge brought the sippy cup to the couch and, whispering again at the cat, compelled it to sniff and rub against the drink, blessing it with whatever powers it had. "And now, Mr. Evan, if you will show me where your arms are, we can begin."

"You need both of them?"

∗◇∗◇∗

Mr. Juge left soon after, well paid for his wasted time but annoyed all the same. He left the gris-gris and a dried chicken's foot. Although he couldn't help Evan with his limbs without all of them present, he listened briefly to Evan's broader set of problems, and told him that if he sacrificed something that was of value to him, and then broke a toe off the chicken's foot, then someone he wanted to hear from would call on him, by phone or in person. Four toes – four people.

Evan opted not to squander them right away, and instead worked through much of the list of phone numbers stored on his phone. It turned out that he had not, tragically, made any friends in the area of the kind that would drop everything to help you navigate the magnified complexities of daily life if your limbs fell off. Some made sympathetic offers to buy him alcohol at an unspecified future occasion. Most agreed that his situation sucked.

Using his teeth, he opened a cabinet and pulled out a coffee mug that an ex-girlfriend had bought for him. Arguably that had some latent sentimental value. He tried dropping it from his mouth to the floor. It hit the carpet and rolled a bit.

With some effort he pushed open his balcony door, and, after checking the sidewalk for pedestrians, let it drop once again. This time the fall was of epic length, practically slow motion, and the mug visibly broke into jagged chunks. Evan felt the thrill of communicating with great powers.

Breaking the chicken toe posed problems. Eventually, after some minor worries about hygiene, he took a toe in his mouth and bit down. It did not break. As hard as he gnawed and twisted and tore, he couldn't wrench one loose.

His phone rang: it was Mr. Juge. "My cat has just produced a hairball, and I have interpreted it. It says you are trying to cheat the chicken foot by breaking something that has no real value to you. It will not work if you do that. I must clean my car seat now. I will send you the bill." And then Mr. Juge hung up.

It was time to call Adriane and ask if she could make her own way from the airport.

❖❖❖

Adriane showered him with sympathy. Then, while she stripped off her smart coat and blouse, she briefly unburdened herself of a few details of her trip and the gracious lift a man had given her from the airport. Before Evan could even begin the required task of learning everything he could about that man in a slow tide of massive jealousy, she was back to the sympathy, and tugging his shirt off to examine his newly-streamlined torso.

"What did the doctor say?" she asked. Evan shared what he knew and, when she asked to see the arms, made a vague suggestion that Mr. Juge had taken one with him as an essential part of his ongoing treatment.

"Well...if he thinks it's a good idea," she said, and then fetched baking soda so she could de-stink the bathtub into which Evan had puked.

Dinner was a feast of frozen pizza and soda drunk from bendy straws. Adriane used a straw in solidarity. When she wanted to make love Evan insisted on having the lights off, and on several occasions she misjudged where she could put her arms and fell forward onto him. He would kiss her whenever she was within range, but he ended up with her hair in his mouth more often than not. Rather than sensual pleasure, he spent long stretches just wondering what kind of ridiculous creature he must look like; some slender, naked otter, undulating on its back.

"Tomorrow's Saturday. We'll try the couch tomorrow," she breathed in his ear after she coaxed an orgasm from him. Passing into sleep, Evan felt, from head to toe, a deep and absolute resentment for everything nice Adriane had done.

DAY EIGHT

Evan gawked at the newspaper. The front page story was about a massive fire in an old downtown building. No one had died – the fire department had even saved a dog. Also on the front page was a story about the local school board discovering unused money in their budget that would pay for new after-school programs to keep The Children out of gangs. Crime was down, employment was up, and some homeless person had responsibly turned in a lost envelope full of cash and been rewarded with a trip to Disneyland.

Adriane couldn't understand why Evan was so angry about it.

She suggested another walk in the park. Evan complied, but spent most of it looking down at the path, grumpily obsessing over what could happen if he were to trip and fall. They made small attempts at cheerful conversation, while the long silences underscored them with a grim and growing pessimism like a low pedal note from an old church organ.

While Adriane professed no medical knowledge, everything Evan had shared about resonant fields and his uncooperative body parts convinced her that it was finally the moment for them to embrace organic and healthy food. He meekly assented, but in the imaginary alternate version of the conversation he overwhelmed her with devastating, unimpeachable arguments about how what makes a man happy is to be able to eat what he damn well wants. He won this imaginary argument several times throughout the afternoon, as he sat through a movie and her making love to him.

DAY NINE

Evan felt like he was proving a point by staying in bed. The point was that sometimes what Adriane needed to do for him was to not do anything. This included cleaning the apartment, which she tried to start doing as he lay there until he growled at her to stop. Eventually, she left, saying that she needed to take care of some things at her place and meet a friend for lunch. She promised to be back for dinner with clothes and supplies for a couple of days' stay.

Evan accepted that there would be time to fight her on that one later. Now his skin was practically crawling from every second that Adriane was still there. Finally, after tying his door key on a string to hang around his neck should he need to go out, she left. He leapt out of bed and got himself cleaned and dressed.

It only took him an hour to get to the café. When he asked to speak with girl-Carl, nobody knew who the hell he was talking about. Changing his description to "the girl with the hair," he was told that Jena didn't work there anymore, man.

Evan hadn't anticipated that.

He raced back home. Sliding open his closet door, he searched through beloved possessions, mentally sorting them by destructibility. There was a jersey from high school (both rippable and flammable), and a ballcap that didn't fit anymore from when his parents had taken the eight-year-old him to Six Flags (ditto, but was he keeping it out of sentiment or habit?).

And there was the necktie.

His last birthday had been his first with Adriane. She had bought him this necktie to wear at the office. He had worn it many times since, so it also represented the old job. By sacrificing this, he would be emphasizing his break from the old, so it not only was good voodoo, it was good psychology.

Gripping it in his teeth, he lowered it into the garbage disposal. The blades became snarled in the threads almost immediately, and the disposal groaned like a creature that was part sea lion and part tuba. But no one would ever wear that necktie again.

This time, the chicken toe broke easily, and Evan, not completely clear how this was supposed to work, announced hesitantly, "Uhhhh girl-Carl...I mean, Jena." Looking sideways apprehensively at his destroyed tie, he wondered if the dark forces with which he had just registered his request knew who he needed.

He stood there in the quiet for a long time. Mr. Juge had only promised that the person he wanted to hear from would contact him. When this would happen had never been specified, and this was just another in the long list of questions throughout his entire life that Evan realized he should have asked when he had the chance.

Then there was a knock at the door. "Come in!" Evan urged, getting more used to that.

It was Girl-Carl. She wore a loose, soft dress over a bathing suit. Evan's eyes collided with her breasts, and he missed the first few words out of her mouth.

"...is the right place. So, like, I don't know if you remember, but I brought you back here the other night and, really, like, I never do this sort of thing, but I saw you had this movie my friends have been bugging me to watch, like forever, so I borrowed it. I figured I'd give it back to you at the coffee-shop but I ended up quitting because they're, like, Objectivists there, and I didn't even know that? So anyway I'm bringing it back now." She extended it towards him, but then stopped on seeing his condition, and, with a meek smile, set it down in the counter. "It's really good. I ripped it," she volunteered.

At last the very urgent thing that he needed to say snapped into focus in Evan's mind. "You have my arm!"

She scrunched up her lips to think about it, and then shook her head. "No, it was in your backpack thing, we brought it in that night. I remember that."

"My other arm!"

Now her lips scrunched up even further. "Oh yeah, you still had an arm on that night. What happened?"

"Resonant fields." Evan prayed she would not ask for further explanation. "It came off in your car."

Now she nodded, and grinned. "It must have been after I gave you the handy. That's my first handy that ever knocked off somebody's arm. That's pretty cool."

There is an affliction to which no man is totally immune: that in nearly all cases, the slightest past sexual contact with a woman renders him instantly persuadable that a mention of sex by her means sex is being offered again. Nearly all his conversational instincts will then bend towards keeping sex as the topic as a means of making the offer a reality.

Taking a suave step forward, Evan asked, "Did you enjoy yourself?"

"To be honest, it was a fun night and all, but overall I think it was me in a really weird self-esteem place. Anyway, I don't have my car right now, it's getting its belts re-belted or something, and my boyfriend's downstairs so I should probably get going. But I can give you my number, I should have the car back by Thursday and then I can get you your arm back. Do you need it for anything right away?"

Evan was still chastened over both the dismissive description of the handy and the apparent rejection of future handies. Stuck for a specific answer, he just said, "It's my arm."

Jena grinned. "It's funny that it's in my car. I feel totally the same way about my car – like, 'what am I going to do without you, car? Ahhhh!'" She scribbled her number on a Post-it by the phone, then gave him a big hug and, with a melodic "Hope you feel better!", pranced out.

As the door clicked shut, Evan's head and torso slipped off his hips and fell onto the floor.

***

Evan had enough screaming in him to get the attention of a neighbor, who very graciously propped him on the sofa with his legs next to him, cleaned the blood from his nose, and provided a wooden spoon he could grip in his teeth to press buttons on the remote or his phone. Then she said a number of prayers in Spanish, and left.

Never before had Evan considered how essential having a complete body was to the act of panicking. With careful strokes of the wooden spoon's handle, he managed to play some soothing music on his phone. Somehow this made his apartment seem even more empty. He looked plaintively at his legs next to him, like he was on a date with them that he knew was going nowhere.

With patience born of necessity, he started searching phone listings for Voodoo experts. He'd made up his mind that Mr. Juge was not only rude and unhelpful, but obviously overcharging for his services. Evan resolved that, once all this was fixed, he would leave a detailed and devastatingly negative online review for Mr. Juge.

He found a large advertisement for "Queen Marie™ and Her Cures," decorated with the picture of a smiling woman in girthsome robes. He called and made a home appointment with their Reservation Priestess, who informed him that the call was being recorded for quality purposes and asked him to acknowledge that he was pursuing alternative cures of his own free will and that he understood that everyone's spirit conduits behaved differently.

The priestess who arrived within an hour was not Queen Marie™, but a fully-certified representative with beautiful cocoa skin, who shared that she did this in order to pay her way to her engineering degree, and that she only accepted cash. Evan, feeling vulnerable, nodded in the direction of his wallet and then told her where to find the one arm he still possessed.

The priestess informed him with something that sounded like regret that the cash he had would only be enough to re-attach the one arm. His legs would have to wait.

With an arm, Evan could operate an ATM, so he saw no flaw in this plan.

Holding a pen in his mouth, he scribbled a mark on several forms, one about the rare but serious side effects of Queen Marie™'s proprietary natural cure-all blend – which included hallucinations and psychosis – and another attesting that Queen Marie™ and Her Cures was not responsible for property lost or stolen during the rare cases when the cure-all blend caused temporary incapacitation, and that Evan was agreeing to waive his right to sue and submit to binding arbitration against the parent company of Queen Marie™ and Her Cures (Patriot Freedom Integrated Solutions) in the case of disputes.

The cure-all sent him off the fucking planet.

DAY TEN

Evan couldn't tell what time it was, though there was daylight coming through the window. He was in his bed, probably thanks to Adriane's help. He remembered only flashes of the trip the cure-all had sent him on: vivid images of his body turning into a waterfall that rained on virgin nymphs and melted their skin off, and a ten-year career with a grizzled unit of wisecracking space commandos tasked with killing the frog beasts of the asteroid belt. And chanting; he remembered ecstatic hordes chanting lyrics from Van Halen songs. Only Hagar-era Van Halen songs.

He rolled over, and felt a lump under him.

He had an arm again.

It was attached, but deadened from lack of circulation. Evan's tongue was too thick to make any joyful sound, but his mind lit up as if from long-missed sunshine. He shook it to life. It moved. It moved at his command!

It didn't really function to the extent that he had taken for granted: it wouldn't bend much at the elbow, the fingers could grip but couldn't flex individually, and the sense of touch was dull. He didn't know if these issues were part of the recovery process or lasting damage from bargain Voodoo. For the moment, he didn't care. He lowered himself from the bed to the floor and, using the arm like a cane, found he could wobble around at a decent speed.

It was well after lunchtime. Adriane had left a curt note sharing that she was at work but had left something for him in the microwave, and that he hoped he could manage to hit the start button.

He ate far more than that. Having an arm was the greatest gift he could want.

He noticed his legs had been moved, and their clothing changed. They now lay sideways on the sofa, wearing his sweat pants over an adult diaper. Another note from Adriane was on them: "FYI – these still poop."

Evan, in a drowsy bloat from food, finally in a moment where he felt the potential for mastery of his circumstances again and so thus could think and reflect like people do, now pictured

Adriane discovering his legs, cleaning them, cleaning the sofa, going out for the diapers...and he felt abysmal. In the face of all her ceaseless support and care he had failed to show gratitude; had failed to even pay her that one daily compliment.

He still needed to get a job, but a higher purpose, a kind of horn call of true manhood, demanded he do something else first. He wrote a text: *Adriane, u r the best fucking girlfriend on history – E.*

He tried jerking off his detached penis; it responded but he felt nothing. But this felt like merely a temporary tragedy. The tide had turned: he was adding body parts rather than subtracting them. Now he could start making it all better, and not a moment too soon. Evan had been thwarted and frustrated and punished in the most capricious ways by the universe, and now he was owed. Now was the time to start collecting.

Reviewing the job inquiries he sent out the previous week, Evan gathered a pile of childhood photographs (the last evidence of a summer at a lake), lit them on fire, broke the second chicken toe, and authoritatively demanded, "Ms. Sawyer in Human Resources." Two hours later, he had a job interview scheduled for Wednesday.

He tried calling for another Queen Marie™ appointment, in the hopes that he could scrounge up the cash to get his legs re-attached. The Reservation Priestess informed him with apologies that, acting in full compliance with federal regulations, they could not provide more than one cure-all in a 30-day period.

He realized he would likely need Adriane's help to get to the interview, and that he had not even checked to see if her work schedule would accommodate this. But she would want this for him; this favor was what all the other favors built to, and if she couldn't do this thing for him, then the other favors meant nothing. He worked hard to tidy himself up before dinnertime and behave with charm.

Adriane seemed weary, but grateful for Evan's newfound attention and optimism. She couldn't deny that Wednesday was going to be a major inconvenience – Evan's eyes flashed at the possibility of betrayal – but she agreed to it, and the rest of the meal passed in discussion of the job and how well Evan would do at it.

He went to sleep with a churning feeling. It was powerful and unruly, but he knew with every fiber he could shape it into what he wanted. It was ironic how closely that shape, that vision of the ideal, resembled exactly what his life had been just two weeks before. After all this, he decided, the lesson was to appreciate what you had.

In the dark around midnight, Evan woke to find the bed empty and his throat dry. Wobbling towards the living room so he could get water from the kitchen, he stopped and gazed at the strangest sight. Adriane, wearing the little silk nightie she hadn't worn for him in three months, was on the couch straddling his lower body. Making love to it.

She heard him, and in the brief moment their eyes met, he saw her crying.

He crawled back into bed without a word.

DAY ELEVEN

Evan pretended to be asleep until Adriane left for work. As soon as he was gone, he made for the living room and scrutinized every inch of his legs. He didn't know what he was looking for: a whiff of her perfume, evidence of climax. He felt a ball of dark, spiky indignance and jealousy swelling within him. Was this all she wanted? He had never fancied himself particularly well muscled or endowed, but was she truly just in it for the sex?

He hated his legs. It was him – his head, his brain, his arm – that had appreciated her at dinner, that had sent the text message telling her how great she was.

His legs looked smug. Evan dragged them off the sofa out of spite. This improved nothing; on the floor they looked insultingly relaxed.

He thought briefly about applying for some more jobs, then talked himself out of it. He didn't know if he could disperse whatever karma might be stored up to help him in this job interview; instead he would focus all his efforts on dominating it.

The most important thing was that he be relaxed and well rested. His arm hadn't improved since yesterday and rest might help that. He resolved to do as little as possible in order to preserve energy, and the TV and beer were his best tools for this.

Adriane was unreasonably critical of how he'd spent his day when she returned. Evan considered himself the bigger man for neither mocking her failure to understand the simple reasoning behind it, nor making any allusion to the way she had demonstrated that she preferred his sex organ to the rest of him. And women were always criticizing men for being sex-obsessed.

He insisted that his legs join him in the bed. Adriane opted to sleep on the couch instead.

DAY TWELVE

Evan had a resume in a folder under his arm and a freshly-pressed shirt with the empty sleeve pinned up. Adriane had noticed but not asked about the destroyed tie. Evan caught a rankling aura of despondency just blaring from her whole person as she picked out a different tie for him.

The drive was mostly silent. Evan clenched his jaw, willing away everything in the universe but the job. Nobody else who came in would be this focused. Nobody else who came in would be this deserving. The job was his. The job was his.

Ms. Sawyer in Human Resources had big round glasses, and peered appreciatively at Evan's resume. Her office was a sanctuary for images of birds – birds on calendars, bird paintings, fat plush birds with impossible smiles lined up on the shelf behind her. A frowning man on a poster cautioned Evan that creating an uncomfortable work environment for women and/or minorities was not cool. A clock ticked and ticked and ticked.

The job fit his skills. And, with some overtime until the first review in six months, the pay would fit his needs. Finally, Ms. Sawyer softly noted that though this was an equal opportunity workplace and that medical conditions were a matter of personal privacy, she was allowing Evan the opportunity to discuss any temporary or permanent conditions that could potentially affect his ability to do the job.

With the stumped end of his torso uneasily balanced on a curved plastic chair, Evan needed his one good arm for steadiness, and so couldn't gesture with it as decisively and assertively as he liked. But he had put a lot of thought into this moment, and rapidly spoke the answer he had committed to memory.

"I'm going to say what everyone in this room's thinking," he began (having prepared his response for the possibility that there would be more than one interviewer). "Here's a guy with no legs and only one arm. You might not be looking for a guy like that. But I want you to picture the future – the future where I'm working for this company, and I've got all my limbs, I've got everything. If you take the time I think you'll see that future's brighter for both of us."

Ms. Sawyer nodded amiably at that. "Since you opened the door, I'm curious: are your limbs going to re-attach? Do you have a timetable on that?"

Evan thought to explain that he would have his other arm back in his possession tomorrow, but realized a split second before speaking that not only was it not relevant, it raised awkward questions. Instead, he just banked on his experience with Queen Marie™ and Her Cures. "I'm on schedule to have everything back in just under 30 days."

Ms. Sawyer gave a matronly grin. "That's truly wonderful. Unfortunately, for this particular position we really are hoping to find someone who can start Monday."

Evan didn't remember much of the rest of the meeting, though he did recall attempting, briefly and clumsily, to re-recite his speech about a brighter future.

✳✳✳

The drive home was even more silent than the one to the interview. Adriane turned on the radio, and an angry voice made endless accusations about the causes of the world's problems. Evan insisted they stop at the drive-through for an ice cream sundae. As they pulled away from the drive-through, the car bounced over a speed bump, and Evan's head, taking part of the neck with it, popped from his body. Adriane caught him by the hair before he hit the ground, though not before he hit the glove compartment, leaving behind a wet smear of the single bite of ice cream he'd managed to put to his lips.

She cradled him in her lap for the rest of the drive. They still didn't speak, and Evan, too furious to even yell, just lay there in her arm, feeling the cotton of her blouse against his cheek, and glared aggressively up at her breasts.

❖

Evan – rather, his head and neck – was set on the couch in front of the TV, with the wooden spoon handy for pressing things, and two tall souvenir glasses on a chair with long straws bent towards his mouth. One contained water, and the other was filled with some protein drink for old people.

He could tilt himself using some muscles in the remaining part of his neck, and even maneuver within a limited space on the couch – although he had an overpowering fear of rolling into the crevice between cushions. So he stared straight ahead at his show on the TV.

He didn't hear what Adriane was saying, but she had her suitcase with her. She set a note by his head, and he resolved to read it at the end of the next episode. He barked a request for her to put the chicken foot by his head. She complied, and then left without another word.

Evan put all his focus into the show; it was entertaining, and it said things about life. People wasting their lives away at jobs had no clue what kind of insights were staring them right in the face if they would just pay more attention to the culture around them. This would be his secret advantage: when it all turned around and things started going his way again, he would blow right by them all because he had taken the time to get insight, to get wisdom. They wouldn't know what hit them, when it all turned around.

The episode was the last one on the DVD. Evan glanced over at the note, saw words like "love" and "always" on it, and grabbed it in his teeth to chew up and swallow. Then he broke another chicken toe, and sullenly spoke Adriane's name. The least that girl could do was come back and change the discs for him.

✧

GOLDEN BROWN

The waffle iron waits. It waits in the dark space under the sink where the spiders dwell, in the bachelor's apartment, the only home it has known since it was pulled from its box long ago. Perched on a thirty-year old crock pot from Mother, behind a crinkling blob of a hundred plastic shopping bags, plug and cord cinched in a sloppy bow, it waits, and thinks.

It does not think about how much time has passed. Days and nights are no different to it, and it has never seen the sun. It does not pass judgment on the lifestyle or eating habits of its owner, because it is incapable of pondering whether its owner eats anything other than waffles. It does not fear the spiders.

Even with all the gifts of modern science the waffle iron can generate but two thoughts, and they are the two thoughts that punctuate and measure its whole life. When not in use it thinks: "Waffle?" That's all. "Waffle?" As if to wonder. "Waffle?" As if to suggest. "Waffle?" As if to present itself ready. And, as the days blend into weeks, "Waffle?" to ever more plaintively signal its loneliness, the plight of anything not allowed to be useful to the world.

Then there is the second thought, which takes over when the waffle iron emerges from its domestic cavern; when it is set upon the counter, fed sweet electricity, pried open in an ecstatic yawn, blasted with cooking spray. Then its thought is affirmative, decisive. "Waffle!" It is the cry of loyalty, the pledge to provide, the total joy of submission to duty.

"Waffle!" A soldier marching to battle. "Waffle!" A nurse seeing the baby's head emerge. "Waffle!" A young banker taking hold of someone's hard-earned money for the first time.

It is an exhilarating thought. The waffle iron fairly tingles with it. When the batter trickles into its cooking grid, oozing and spreading through the little angular canyons, had its designers shown the foresight to equip it in this way the waffle iron would blush, it so forgets itself with excitement.

For these minutes, the waffle iron is fully itself. It is committed, it is fervent, it is relieved of all doubt and anguish. It is religious, it is romantic, it is suffused with absolute belonging. It serves up its treasure, light and crisp and sweet, and asks no thanks or reward. It lives for the chance to give.

They are so brief, these moments of "Waffle!" And, especially as it is owned by a dedicated bachelor, they may not come for months at a time. It may spend cruel, teasing days on the counter by the sink – untended and uncleaned – before being shoved back into its home in the dark. It is a sparse diet of happiness.

One might fancy, when the door is opened to the cupboard under the sink, when light spills across its face, that the interrogative "Waffle?" might take on the tiniest urgency. No one has ever determined if this is true or simply sentiment. All that is known is that it will ask the question until it is answered, or until it can cook no more.

And while we were tuned in to this frequency, we might hear an unconscious syncopation from nearby. For while the waffle iron carries on its high and eager questioning from within the cupboard, it is not alone. Beneath it, one leg standing forever in a tiny rusty puddle, sits the crock pot, the thirty-year-old one from Mother, and it also asks the void if its services will be needed.

It has waited much longer, but has borne it with sturdy patience. There is a self-assurance to these machines, because to be there, and to never be used, is unimaginable. The assumptions that idea would violate are too much to ask of them, with their two-thought limit.

The crock pot's voice is lower, more soothing, promising warmth on the cold, rainy nights, sustenance for the hungry. "Stew?" it asks. It takes its time and treasures the sound – "Steeeeewwwwwwww?" It is the sound of a beckoning embrace, a nanny breathing a nonsense song to a baby as it falls asleep.

It can make more than stew, and will go about it with the same nourishing satisfaction. But it treats every meal inside it as if it were broth and meats and cut vegetables and spices, like a parent with many children that loves all and favors none. When "Stew?" becomes "Stew!" the satisfaction radiates into the room, full and resonant. Even if the crock pot could speak another thought, it wouldn't contemplate it.

Waffle and stew, waffle and stew. Like frogs in the nighttime, making their own curtain of sound. But they cannot hear one another, and we cannot hear either. We hear only the occasional stretch of those plastic bags, and a drip of water from a leak the bachelor will someday discover.

✳✳✳

III. DREAMS

"Do you see the story? Do you see anything? It seems to me I am trying to tell you a dream – making a vain attempt, because no relation of a dream can convey the dream-sensation, that commingling of absurdity, surprise, and bewilderment in a tremor of struggling revolt, that notion of being captured by the incredible which is the very essence of dreams..."
– Joseph Conrad

"'That's how it is with dreams,' said Priscilla. 'They're the perfect crime.'"
– Tom Robbins

TOURIST TRAP

The sign advertised the train museum as six miles north of the main highway. Off the wide concrete these were slow, hot miles. The air buzzed with insects. The road rose and fell gently; not hills or even bumps, just waves of land, lulling me as I drove. Farm sprinklers – wheeled, industrial – perched over the land feeding it from long metal arms, like giant mother birds.

I found the building – low and wide, concrete and dark wood – sitting, humble and square and calm, on its appointed patch; surviving weather, surviving disinterest. My car tires sliced through the gravel of the parking lot, throwing up pebbles. I cut my engine.

Silence

A whitewashed wooden square stood along the path; an old long oval hung over the door. Both made the same announcement – *Train Museum* – in simple red letters. The square sign had more to say, in the same slender hand-made letters: *See the history of the train rendered in these world-famous models!*

I felt an instinct to look around me, but mine was still the only car in the parking lot, six miles north of the main highway.

That radiant sunlight left me dazed and blinking as I stepped through the door. But my pupils widened, and the room emerged in my vision like the center dot of an old television, all light and color blossoming from one point to fill a black void – a simple lobby (not eight feet by eight), where a rack of postcards proudly flanked an American flag. And here was the woman: smiling, awaiting me.

Her squint and smile were like creases in fresh bread. Small and plump, flowers on her shirt, traces of what must have been a buttercup shade in her simple white bob. I thought she could have stepped right out of the wallpaper. They had not always known each other, but they belonged to one another now, sure, like roosters and barns, berries and cream.

"Welcome to the Museum," she said. She produced a brochure. "This is the Model Train Exhibit, telling the history of the train. The displays are interactive, they are fun for the whole family. Try pressing the buttons you see along the way for surprises. Admission is a five-dollar donation, and please do sign our guestbook at the end, tell us where you come from and where you're going."

She stood back now and her smile spread. For a moment I couldn't move.

"Enjoy the tour," she said at last, and I noticed I'd been holding my breath. I stepped into the horseshoe corridor.

Display cases ran along both walls, closed off by windows of durable plastic. I felt, more than heard, the buzz of fluorescence. Worn carpet rolled ahead of me, taking a sharp right out of vision at the far end, calling like a forest trail.

And behind the clear plastic, the trains made their steady rounds.

Trains from every age crossed lakes of blue paint, and burrowed through plaster mountains with only a tiny bulb to light their way. Without trepidation or triumph they whirred through the same loop they'd whirred through three minutes before, and would again three minutes hence. They did not stop for passengers, nor the old model of a coal chute sitting on toothpick-thin legs. Dauntless, humming unperturbed, they carried all the fuel and passengers they would ever want.

Following its own program, the light dimmed and made a nightfall. Streetlamps winked on in model towns. A dignified gray lighthouse cast a guiding spot towards ships that would never come in: they were painted on the back walls. The trains stayed true to course and speed, and soon their constructed world gave them daylight again.

I paused at a placard by a miniature station, a simple old platform crowded with figurines in fancy dress, top hats the size of a cat's nose. They stood in jubilant poses. The placard read:

When a son of the Maffit family of Chicago fell in love with a daughter of the Hovey family of Lincoln, it was decided to hold the wedding on a train line that ran between the cities so that the families would each make a trip to the other's home. The celebration lasted three days, time enough to spark a deep affection between two more members of the families. The families disembarked at the Lincoln station, leaving bride and groom to their honeymoon in the mountains of Colorado. In forty-six years of marriage, they never rode a train separately.

So many words squeezed onto that placard, and yet the letters seemed to stretch and swell in my vision as I read them, as if straightening up with pride. Night fell on the Maffit and Hovey families. It did nothing to quiet their celebration.

The train tracks ventured into a brown desert, and I followed them. Towering rocks stood sentry along their path, and the rear wall was painted a brilliant blue. A metal button poked out of the display towards me, like a small bud. I pressed it, and a trail of bulbs made the impression of a shooting star, a present for travelers far from the lights of home.

I waited for daylight, and then pressed it again. It was invisible now, and yet I knew it had happened. It gave me a strange comfort.

On a side track one train idled, intentionally still.

On an unseasonable day in March of 1933, a train was stranded here by foreboding conditions in the Rocky Mountains ahead. This was no tragedy to Virginia Newkirk, who prayed for every extra second that could be added to her journey east, that she might hold her daughter Helen longer before having to deliver her to the care and schooling of more solvent relatives. To relieve her boredom, twelve-year old Helen danced in the aisle, singing a song she had heard on the radio to the delight of the passengers. One of them was the newly-hired agent of a music publishing company that was expanding operations into Kansas City. He persuaded the Newkirks to exit the train early, and Helen spent the next thirty years singing songs and commercial jingles for a fair income on radio and, eventually, television.

Other trains zipped mindlessly by this one, where the Newkirks, somewhere inside, remained frozen in their moment of dread turning to deliverance.

The tracks betrayed no geographical reason. A Western desert could melt into an Atlantic fishing village, yet the train somehow escaped to surge across a nearby miniature of the Mighty Mississippi. Mountains neighbored oceans, and the metal cities did not swallow the villages, but shared equally in the electric light of the fake sun and stars while the little trains wove and purred. There was no measure of miles, no borders.

I pressed another button by a plain of grass, and from a plastic shrub a coyote head poked out to look for the moon.

Roy Caffrey had a way of not shedding despair, though others had found the path forward from tragedies like his. He could learn a lesson, but the regret and anger of the mistake remained. And when he could find people to love, the melancholy of those lost would still not stop visiting. He had no one to rage at for the illness which grew inside him, and he knew too well there would be no justice in it. Heavy with drink, he passed out while following this track in Nebraska and didn't feel himself die.

The corridor bent twice now, making the bottom of a U-shape, and here the trains circled a great park with a lake bounded by sand and grass, a bandstand, and a Ferris wheel. Here the stringed lights never dimmed, and the pony rides ran all night. Family figures stood mid-gallop on the fairway, balloons always plump and inflated, pink dots of cotton candy always just beyond their lips.

And within this park, the tiny model children rode a tiny model train, round and round a tiny model track.

An abundant row of buttons offered themselves to my control. With a touch I could light the top of a maypole. I could turn the carousel. Electric fireworks blossomed, and rowboats circled through an intimate cave.

There was no placard here, no story to tell except the fair itself: its hope, with paint and filament, to trick music into the ears and sugar onto the tongue. The trains rolled by it, stoic.

I followed them around the last bend, that scuffed and frayed carpet drawing me back now towards the lobby. The trains skirted works of man: mining pits and diners. They bridged a high and rocky gorge over a painted river.

On a hot night in August of 1952, a handful of men, in a desperate fever of anger, conspired to seize a porter known only as Isaac over a perceived advance on one of their wives. They threw him out of the train over this gorge, and what became of him was never known. One of the co-conspirators, after many tormented nights, turned to the service of the Lord. It is not known whether he found forgiveness, but twelve years later he was jailed.

At last I reached the train yard, a thick weave of tracks aimed at every horizon. In this nervous center were cars and engines and switches, and my mind reeled at so many combinations and destinations. As trains glided in from their little odysseys, I could loop them around the yard, delaying their next departure.

As I let one slip free, I thought of the intersections behind me, and wondered if, with my nudge of timing, I had created an inevitable catastrophe for the days or weeks ahead. I wondered if the owners of the train museum knew these paths and their timing well enough to anticipate it, wipe it away. I surprised myself with the force of my hope that this was so.

Then, poised on a junction track aimed out into that vast adventure, I saw a ready train. At its far back end, on the little jutting platform of its caboose, was a figure, the first I had seen on any of the trains, sitting, legs dangled over the ground through the railing. Like the other model people I'd seen it was too small for any but the most suggestive features; it could have been man, woman, boy, girl. The figure and the train waited together, and I could not see if they were eager or wistful, anxious or bold or serene.

Now the corridor ended, and an old banner thanked me. Two machines promised to sell me a fat gumball or stamp my pennies with the symbol of the world-famous train museum. On a simple stand, titled in fancy script, was the guestbook. I pulled it open by a purple marking ribbon.

Every page encouraged me to sign, and I saw that people had not just left their names. They wrote of loves lost and found, dead brothers, great ambitions, beloved buildings that grew grander in the memory for each year since their demolition, the miracles of spring and the cruelty of old scars. Some pages showed faded spots, the ghosts of teardrops.

I took the pen and wrote:

It has been 10,000 miles since I slept in my own bed. I can go home now.

And I walked out the door into the blazing afternoon.

※◇※

SWAYGRON JEP: INSURANCE MAN
FROM PLANET TWELVE

The great guns of the pirate lord Pakalo's fleet trained onto the small space cruiser christened the *Durban*. Freshly arrived through the nearest light-portal, the *Durban* flashed diplomatic colors from its running lights, and, to underline its utter lack of provocation, broadcast everything from friendly greetings in all languages to the kill code that would allow the pirate fleet to seize its environmental controls, empty it of oxygen, and murder everyone on board; this being considered the very latest in fashionable obsequity.

Swaygron Jep heard the announcement of their arrival in his small cabin. As per procedure, he checked his tank. His office required him to keep a portable oxygen supply for the estimated 3.4% possibility that the pirates would use the kill code in order to test the *Durban*'s sincerity. But they didn't, so Jep grabbed his actuarial pad, flicked a speck off his boots, and departed for the command bridge.

The *Durban*'s captain was on the command bridge, patiently communicating their purpose – to transport ransom and tribute for the Mighty Pakalo, in return for which, if it suited Mighty Pakalo, he would relinquish the stolen Brick belonging to the colony of Lucida Anseris Prime. Swaygron compared the conversation against the Brick negotiation conversation protocols his company had approved, and rated the Captain's conformity (within the tolerance built in to the algorithm for the necessities of sometimes bluffing with pirates) in real-time. This triggered a beautiful cascade of mathematical adjustments to the estimated payout for Lucida Anseris Prime in the event of Full Brick Loss.

In the early days of colonization, hardy pioneers would actually land on unexplored planets and gut out a foothold there. But while the margins on empty planet real estate were astounding for speculators, and a large class of people romantically considered themselves potential explorers of exactly this type, few of them ever signed up for such expeditions: they invariably involved grubbiness and mass death.

The security and comforts such hardy would-be migrants expected required a supply of rare minerals that would take decades of planet-bound mining and industry to locate and process locally. To resolve this paradox, colony start-up firms invented The Brick – a ready-made supply of rare minerals, calculated down to the microgram, which could take all the primitivism out of the adventure to a wild and untamed world.

Brick Colonies hence became attractive and lucrative expansions of civilization, but Bricks themselves became an attractive target for daring thieves, since they were both small, and, by definition, the single most valuable item on their respective worlds. You couldn't buy and transport a Brick without Brick Insurance, and only the insurance companies of Planet Twelve, like Jep's, offered it.

❊❊❊❊

The pirates disdainfully broke off conversation for the third time, and then fired a few petty shots at the *Durban*'s engines. Swaygron checked his probabilities and saw that he likely had another half-hour before someone in authority on the pirate side got bored and the next phase could begin. He went to check on Wrightman Duncan.

Duncan was taking off his clothes in the cargo hold, the better to squeeze himself into a space burial coffin. He had spent most of the day cunningly altering it to include a small propulsion system. The Hero Option was a very cost-effective approach to Brick Retrieval when successful; of course, it was rarely successful. Still, the settlers of Lucida Anseris Prime had selected the Hero Option with their policy, and Duncan came with good references, the best of all being that he was still alive.

"So...it's the bean-counter," announced Duncan with a blend of jocularity and contempt. "Count any good beans today?" In the certification courses Jep had attended to prepare for Hero encounters, there was extensive time devoted to their conversational quirks, and reminders to not take anything they said or did personally. The trainers, working from scripts, never quite got the nuances right, though.

Jep gave a politely sheepish grin and proceeded to give the coffin a cursory once-over. "Sure you can fit in there, Mr. Duncan?"

"Mister is for the fancy people who get to sleep at night because of people like me, bean-counter. Just call me Duncan."

Jep noted that Duncan's eyes flicked on multiple occasions to the small pile of outer clothing he had shed and was leaving on the floor, and decided that Duncan probably wanted to talk about them. "Of course, Duncan. Are you removing your clothing in order to better fit inside this...vessel?"

"Sure am. Not even room for weapons." Duncan rolled his shoulders and clenched his fingers a few times. "Some days, no matter what your fancy governments do, your own hands are all you've got to rely on. Looks like this is one of those days." Jep's review of the coffin's interior confirmed that there was in fact enough room for Duncan to be fully-clothed if he chose, but there was an acknowledged and eternal gulf between the logical processes of insurance men and Heroes, and Jep was under no mandate to bridge that gulf today.

Jep offered his hand. "My employers, myself, and all the colonists of Lucinda Anseris Prime wish you luck." He knew that Duncan's chances of success were somewhere below 1.8%, but given such rarity, a single occasion of success could increase the attractiveness and profit margins of Hero Options dramatically and prevent the necessity of a payout, so Jep was as sincere in his wishes as he knew how to be.

Duncan stuck his chin up and put his fists against his hips. "Luck is for cowards and collectivists, bean counter," he declared with a stirring timbre. "But I repeat myself. I'd love a good-bye kiss. So unless you want to be the one to give it to me, you'd better go send Estrella down here."

"Estrella," Jep knew, was actually Crewperson Shentok, who worked in Sensory Analysis. She had accepted a bonus of three weeks paid shore leave to pose as a disenfranchised Princess and congress no less than twice with Wrightman Duncan during his passage to the negotiation. It was an entirely reasonable contract rider Duncan's agent had arranged for, and Crewperson Shentok was allowed to keep the provided wardrobe.

Jep left the cargo hold. He had accomplished his objective, which was to ascertain via a discreet scanner in his palm the chemical balance in Duncan's brain right before his departure and make it available to compare with his recorded profile in the after-mission report. Some Heroes had a tendency to improvise various combinations of stimulants and relaxants leading up to their missions, feeling that this optimized their performance. To Jep's unceasing amazement, 7.6% of the time they were actually correct.

◇

The pirates had taken several more shots at non-essential areas of the ship. This slotted in well with the plan, as the Captain could claim the attack had caused a fatality, allowing the launch of the coffin to proceed. Jep hoped that Duncan and Crewperson Shentok had enjoyed sufficient parting time together; he had held a few conversations with Shentok during the trip and found her to be very pleasant company.

The Captain by now had worked his way up to a parlay with Most Terrible Viscount Jagan Kir, who at least had managerial authority in Pakolo's hierarchy. As Jep returned to the bridge, the Most Terrible Viscount was in the middle of an impressively florid description of Pakolo's many achievements in piracy, and how this made the Captain's most recent offer just one crucial sliver away from a mortal insult. It may have been malnourishment from his long duty shift, or the fact that Kir had decorated his formal armor with human spines, but the Captain began to plead and grovel well outside acceptable parameters. Jep quietly clucked with disapproval, and, with an expulsion of breath, duteously flagged the deviant behavior.

Kir offered one hour to acquiesce to his latest demands, and switched off his transmission. Jep approached the Captain, who was slumping in his command chair.

"Captain, I need to inform you that you have already raised your offer to 82% of the maximum approved ransom. Our protocols only allow you to offer 78% during an encounter with a Gamma-Level authority."

The Captain pursed his lips with plaintive exhaustion. "That was a Gamma-Level?"

"Oh yes. You don't remember his name in the briefing packet?"

"He said he was Pakolo's most celebrated and trusted warrior. That sounded like at least Beta-Level."

"And you believed him?"

"He had *bones* on his armor!"

Jep sighed, and tried to sympathize. These situations put a tremendous strain on captains, and Jep had a small amount of discretion in cases like this. "Would you say you are under unusual stress right now?"

The Captain ruefully shook his head. "You mean besides trying to keep my crew safe and prevent the collapse of an entire colony?"

This next bit had to be handled delicately, and Jep hoped the Captain would catch the nuance. "I mean have you or a loved one been recently diagnosed with a fatal or near-fatal malady? Have you recently met any previously unknown family members that you are struggling to connect with? Your report on this negotiation is, of course, your own responsibility. I am merely suggesting as a courtesy that you review this optional form that might...contextualize your circumstances." Jep then transferred a blank of his company's Standardized Form for Medical, Familial, and Idiosyncratic Short-Term Stress Modifiers to the Captain's command pad.

His bosses discouraged this sort of behavior, and maybe Jep sometimes erred on the compassionate side, but his efforts usually came to naught regardless. Captains who could check many boxes on the SF-MFISTSM without the slightest fudging or rhetorical gymnastics would still refrain from using it most of the time. Jep always assumed this had something to do with the Honor of Command and other notions that cost otherwise sensible people far more around the margins than they often realized. Still, he had done what was permitted, and so left the Captain alone with whatever thoughts captains have in such moments. Jep was in the mood for a light meal.

✳✷✳

Jep read some combative opinion pieces from the news services as he munched on mineral/protein constitutes in the mess. He found that he enjoyed their flavor better early in the mission before they had been recycled too many times through the crew's digestive systems and back into the yeast pools. He preferred his wife Roselet's cooking, but something about the soft tang and small servings of the constitute rations reminded him that he was in the midst of excitement. As if on cue, the ship shook and rumbled from another barrage of temperament from Pakalo's fleet.

He wondered how Wrightman Duncan was doing. His plan, as near as Jep understood, was to drift via the most minute and undetectable manual thrust adjustments to the hull of the fleet's capital ship. Duncan claimed to have once been held captive on one "just like it," and therefore knew its rough layout and security systems. He then intended to cut his way into an unoccupied area of the ship and, via a combination of fisticuffs, hostage-taking, and his gamble that "an old buddy" might be working in the pirates' mess, gradually acquire an arsenal of weapons and access codes while sabotaging crucial systems.

His assumption was that Pakolo would keep the Brick on the ship out of the irrational covetousness and object fetish for which pirates were known, and that he could find its location before the crew became aware of his presence. Failing that, he would simply brawl with everyone on the command bridge, overpower them, and set a self-destruct countdown while behaving in a manner "just crazy enough" to convince the pirates he would kill them all and himself if they did not meet his demands.

Jep had to admit that this was all very sophisticated by Hero planning standards.

One of the luxuries available in the *Durban*'s stores was a small helping of tea leaves from a planet to which Jep had holidayed with his wife five years before. To his great pleasure, he found that a cup was affordable within his per diem.

✳✳✳

Most Terrible Viscount Jagan Kir was in the midst of a vigorous and boastful rant on the viewscreen as Jep, summoned inconveniently midway through his tea, re-entered the bridge. On the floor of the pirates' bridge lay the beaten form of Wrightman Duncan. Despite the subtle distancing effect of the viewscreen, Jep never failed to find human blood in such volume distressing.

Kir was explaining that the cargo hold Duncan had attempted to enter surreptitiously had actually been converted (shockingly, against the manufacturer's safety codes) to the crew's recreational quarters, and many of the off-duty pirates had been there in the midst of a spirited Bludgeon match when Duncan had sliced a tiny hole in their wall and slid through it into the room.

Jep, actuarial pad at the ready for voice recording, whispered to the Captain: "Can you attest that Mr. Duncan, known also as the Mission Hero, is deceased in body and/or brain function?" Just then, however, he saw Duncan's body stirring, and so backed away with an apologetic cough.

Duncan's torso lurched up from the ground, while his arm pawed seemingly blindly in the direction of a control panel. Quickly, one of the pirates knocked him back to the ground, and two more kicked him where he lay, apparently to amuse themselves.

His voice a ragged wail, Duncan shouted, "The world will always make way for the man who is truly free!" Then Kir stomped on his skull, crushing it into a mass of pulp and bone chunks. Jep noted the time and made the appropriate updates to the mission report.

He stepped back up the Captain's ear. "By my calculations, you are now authorized to offer up to but not exceeding 88.5% of the maximum approved ransom. Best of luck." He was confident this would cheer the Captain. Things would be resolved in a matter of hours, and while Swaygron Jep was not a betting man, he found himself hopeful that the Brick would be recovered. Not to mention that the life insurance policy his company had purchased on Wrightman Duncan would cover an appreciable chunk of the mission expenses. Hero Insurers were so optimistic – Jep couldn't fathom how they stayed in business.

❖

Planet Twelve was not the twelfth planet of any system, and it circled no twelfth star. It had been founded by a consortium of financial traders who worshipped an order known as The Twelve. Believers in The Twelve knew that rules in society were little more than shackles and blood drains built by the weak to cripple the strong out of petty jealousy and feelings of sexual inadequacy, so a society built around the fewest possible rules would be, by definition, the most virtuous. Its founders had articulated twelve such inviolable, unalterable rules, and all agreed this had the coincidental advantage of being a strong sounding number.

Planet Twelve was their colony, and The Twelve were to be its only laws. The early years were bumpy: when one tycoon decided to serve organic meat at a summer party at his private land mass, an envy-driven craze for agriculture led to the swift importation of an entire sub-class of real meat animals and their uppity caretakers, which was then followed by several gruesome and embarrassing breakouts of food poisoning at the height of the social season. Fortunately, the chieftains of Planet Twelve soon discovered a previously unknown but in no way contradictory codicil to The Twelve that allowed for a quality inspection and certification regime, provided that the all the inspectors signed a pledge to live by Twelvish principles in all their financial and sexual dealings.

The insurance industry, too, had once been forbidden, as the mightily-fortified followers of The Twelve saw it as unconscionable that they should subsidize every fool who went through life unprepared for the consequences of their own foolishness. Eventually, though, yet another revealed and praised amendment to The Twelve permitted the creation of the best educated and compensated class of insurers in the entire cluster, and it was considered to be the gravest sign of naïveté to draw any connections between this revision and the proximate destruction of a resident's private lake resort via large meteor.

Most insurance men of Planet Twelve enjoyed long and comfortable careers ingeniously thwarting title claims filed by the many bastards that local titans sired among the help. But Swaygron Jep had felt a certain restless stirring in him almost from the moment he finished his certification courses, and even now that stirring which inspired him to the field of Brick Insurance took him off-planet for as much as two to three weeks on occasion, attending these enviable adventures among the blastdogs of the wildest regions. They made him a figure of great popularity at the home office.

As his transport glided towards the atmosphere, Swaygron took real pride in the final approach. He watched out the portal and anticipated the sights he had seen on the way to so many landings at the public spaceport: the vast jungles, the vaster artificial jungles, the imposing sealed domes of Hoffclo's Freeland, and finally Swaygron's home island, where resident employees who had yet to be approved for property ownership were permitted to rent in a block of apartments surrounded by an acidic lake in sparkling emerald green, as well as the network of volcanoes engineered to channel all seismic activity away from the better-appraised areas of Planet Twelve. Anyone who lived on Booter Island would tell you that the sunsets were the envy of their betters. With no irony, he hummed the great martial Anthem of The Twelve.

His datanode synchronized with the home network, and Swaygron saw to his joy that, by the time the spacecraft had been decontaminated and all its passengers shown the required

Twelvish re-education dramavid, it would be past quitting time locally, and he would be able to skip the office and go home.

And so Swaygron Jep ended his day in his own grav-field bed, his body caressed into a relaxing alignment by the most dense and precise array of lev-springs that could be produced by the masterful mattress makers of Planet Twelve. He looked over at his wife, Roselet Jep, and considered suggesting sex to her. But she seemed pretty involved with her book, so he passed into sleep, and dreamt sane dreams.

❖

PAPER BALL

Sister walks into the party in Brother's cozy loft apartment. They are so alike, Brother and Sister, but he has the littlest extra courage that has won him friends and success. Everything in the room is an emblem of this difference. He has decorated it with taste in every available spot.

Clever people wear good clothes at the party. It is devastating. They are drinking and talking and they are talking and drinking and they have not noticed Sister. They do not mean to do this, it is just that there is a kind of looking they have given up entirely.

But tonight Sister carries a large ball of crumpled paper, or maybe some moist and pulpy stuff that has not yet evolved into paper. She pauses by a woman in a short, dark dress. She summons all her willpower and asks for the woman to look at the paper ball. When the woman looks, it has changed, a side is gone and you can see inside. A squarish shape sits there, like a box inside an eggshell. It looks like a little building, revealed within the paper ball.

Sister has not moved her hands. She has not dropped nor squeezed nor torn the paper ball. It has simply become this shape.

Suddenly Sister is fascinating.

The woman in the short, dark dress reaches out. When she touches the paper it changes again, crinkling and folding and crushing in upon itself until that suggestion of the building has become all that it is. It is, in perfect detail, the shape of the restaurant down the street.

"I need to eat something!" shouts the woman in the short, dark dress, and she leaves the loft right away. Brother is bothered that the party has fewer guests.

The little paper restaurant drops from Sister's hands and turns over and over, rolling itself back into a ball. It rolls across the floor, up and over furniture, until it rolls right up her body to rest back in her arms. And now everyone wants to touch it. They cannot remember ever wanting anything else.

The party is over. Sister tells Brother this paper ball will make them rich. Brother believes her. He wants to know if there are others that they could sell. For a single second, she has a flash of fantasy of using it to make more of its kind. And the paper ball instantly unwraps itself and swallows her.

It covers her from head to toe. When it peels off of her, time has passed and she does not know how much. Her skin has become pouchy and greenish. In front of her the pulpy folds of the paper wrap themselves into a form. For a moment so fast she must work the rest of her life to hold it in memory, she sees it take the form of a baby, pink and perfect. And then it is a paper ball again, and it divides in two, and the twin to the first drops to the floor and rolls out the door and soon it finds a buyer who will pay anything to have it feed their wishes.

The paper ball swallows Sister again and again, and makes more of itself and makes them rich. There is always a cost, though: she is becoming stooped and heavy and sallow and weary and sad.

They buy luxuries to stuff into Brother's little loft. But Sister barely recognizes Brother anymore – he took a paper ball for himself and revealed to it that since childhood he had yearned, no, needed, to become a dragon. And so it made him a dragon, twenty feet long and proud and covered in blue scales. Only he cannot go out to feed for fear of being shot from the sky. So he stays in the loft, cramped and curled into a great bed, morose and starved and too timid to breathe that he might burn his own pretty belongings.

She always keeps one paper ball for herself, but has lost count of how many have dropped to the floor and rolled out the door. She sits across Brother's chest as he struggles on the great bed with no fire left in his lungs. She shakes him by the head, and insists, "I will take care of us. I will take care of us.

"With the paper ball."

✳✳✳

BUBBLES

My father is in physics; well, I mean to say he studies physics. It's his business to study it. We're all IN physics, if you catch me.

He works up at the lab. I haven't seen him in a while, but how can you begrudge that of someone working on such important things?

I never caught on with science. I guess that means I'm more like my mother, God rest her. I don't get what happens in the world through numbers and tests, but if you tell it to me like a joke, I get it all the way. It's why I've always enjoyed living in this town. This place is hilarious.

I'll tell you a story that counts as a joke around here; it happened to my father back when I was a child. He was in a test chamber at the lab, and he and this partner he's always talking about – I never met him but I guess he was Dad's best friend – were drinking mugs of coffee and talking about the universe. This is something they had to do professionally, but it rubbed off into their everyday talk, too.

Dad was saying there's a whole other universe out there made up of all the things we don't know. But his friend said that we were just one universe, equal to an infinite number of others that were all equally unknown. So if you wanted to be mathematically clever you could say that if you average that out then it means we'll never actually know anything at all. Pretty smart folks, to come up with things like that.

And then there was this queer pop in the air, and they looked over and each of them had a second mug of coffee. Just like that – identical mugs, coffee the same temperature, even the same amount of sugar my dad puts in.

That's not the funny part; things like that were known to happen at the lab. But they both looked at the extra mugs, then looked at each other, and they said: "This just proves my point." And they said it at the same time.

That's the funny part.

I'm sure they told you all about the neighborhood, but this whole area is near the lab, and that has had a definite effect on the way life goes. They mentioned the bubbles, right? A few years after they started doing whatever it is they do up there, the whole area ended up with these bubbles. They called them by some other word but some of us got to calling them bubbles and that's what stuck.

They're not physical bubbles. Maybe physics bubbles? Somebody smarter than me can answer that. But most likely you'd just say they're bubbles of time, settled all over town. Slow time over here, fast time over there. You can't see them: the scientists had to march around with stopwatches and map out where they appeared, and if they know where the bubbles came from they haven't told us. My father tried to explain it to me once, but all I can tell you is they're a side product of some experiment into the fundamentals of things.

After a while, you'll start to know when you go in or out of one; you feel a little queasy and there's this quiet ache down deep in your muscles. It passes after a bit. The Government made a pill: they don't make you take it, but it takes a lot of the edge off. I think it's thinning out my hair, but you make your trades in life.

The time difference isn't so big, maybe a second per minute. Meals don't line up at first and little things like that, but after a while even the big things start to get out of whack.

My neighbor, his house is in fast time. Look over at his window sometimes and he's earlier out of bed each day. Didn't happen that much faster than everywhere else. You look directly at it, it seems normal enough. But boy is it funny, watching a life in fast time over the long haul. The Government offered to move him to another house if he didn't want to live faster. He refused. "If only you people," he said, "could feel what it's like for someone like ME to slow down."

Most people don't know what he means by that. They argue about whether he means to say it's a torment or a kind of ecstasy. I get it though – I know he means both.

My house is right in the middle of a slow bubble. It's been here forty years. Even in my neighborhood – which anyone would confess has got its peculiarities – to see a fast bubble and a slow bubble all but sharing a property line is a dooze of a peculiarity. Sometimes I think it's why my father bought it; no matter how many hours there are in a day, he's curious in all of them. I know Mom never liked it.

In my slow bubble, the world outside looks like it's in an unhealthy rush. But I can just sit and listen to the kettle whistle. I sleep more. No one gets to tell me I spend too much time with the Sunday crossword. The old lady down the street used to leave her pies here – said they'd keep longer!

It's better if you don't spend too much time on the phone; it sounds strange. Go see someone, that's what we do around here.

If you've got kids, you should know they moved the school to make sure it was in an area without bubbles. It seemed like the fair thing to do. There's a bit of bubble that spills over into one of the parks; not the one by the lake, the other one. First they just marked it with cones, but then somebody got the idea to plant trees around it. The way they blossom and turn out of order, it's something. Green on one side and the autumn gold on the other – that's what happens to my favorite one in August these days.

I feel like I see my kids less, because I live slow. They wanted to get out of the neighborhood when they grew up and they made it. More of my friends are drifting away too: life is taking them places at a pulse I just don't feel. I used to get at least ten hours of normal time a day from going to work, but a couple of years ago I started to work at home. Too much normal time made me seasick. That's the only way I know how to describe it.

And there's the waiting. Sometimes it's sweet to wait, but other times...I'll probably live longer than most of the people I know. I'll probably die the last of us.

I'll tell you another joke about that lab of my father's. He took me on a tour once, and we walked by an office. There was this perfect little desk in there, and a little boy who looked about six years old was scribbling furiously at this giant math problem that took up the whole back wall.

"Who's that?" I couldn't help but ask.

And my dad said, "Oh, that's the old man. The stuff he works on...I don't even understand it."

Now you're going to think I'm goofy, but I could swear that six-year old was a dead ringer for a picture I've got of my father at that age. That's the best way I know how to tell you what kind of neighborhood you're moving into.

They never did tell me if he died or not. He just went in to work one day, and didn't come back. From then on, whenever we asked after him they just said, "He cannot leave the lab right now." That's all they said from that day on: "He cannot leave the lab right now." At least I know he's got plenty of coffee the way he likes it there.

✴✴✴

AUDIO BONUS

Enjoy a dramatic reading of "Bubbles" by veteran film/TV actor John Walcutt at the award-winning audio drama podcast *Earbud Theater*. Search and subscribe on iTunes or go directly to: http://earbudtheater.com/ and find the episode in the Podplay Index.

✴✴✴

HOMAM, THE VERY HELPFUL GENIE

"It would be like a virtual reality place, only everything would look and feel completely real. But it wouldn't be real real. Have you heard of virtual reality?"

Homam the Genie most certainly had not heard of virtual reality. He had just spent eighty-seven years sequestered in a soldier's old metal flask locked away in a trunk, the traditional lamp not being available at the time. But it was simple enough to reach out into the chatter of the world and grab enough to go on. Telepathy was essential for Genies – you needed to catch up on the culture and the language somehow. Much had changed during his slumber, superficially speaking. Apparently virtual reality was a manufactured illusion for the senses, false surroundings wherein people could experience things without danger or moral quandary. A place to be full master of one's dreams. Homam immediately saw the appeal. But now Master continued.

"Only I don't want it to be in a fixed place, or be super-heavy so I have to lug it around. Like, I could flip over to it whenever or wherever I am. I don't know how you'd do that. Like a helmet maybe?"

That suggestion hung in the air a moment. Master leaned forward on a couch and rubbed his hands together self-consciously.

Homam gathered himself into a more opaque form and spoke now, in a timbre tuned down from the bombast he used ceremonially. "You want a space that exists outside of normal space." Master nodded eagerly. "One you can enter at will, and inside you would conjure up your desires in exact detail in privacy."

Master seemed to be waiting for more, so Homam punctuated his announcement by twirling his beard and summoning up a little ethereal jangling noise.

Master's face brightened, even flushed a little – he was picturing the wish already. This pleased the genie. Many of his brethren were cynical and cruel, and lived to trick their masters by executing their wishes in a way that punished them. Irony – genies were suckers for irony, and Homam had played at that game in his youth. But over the millennia he had found real pride and fulfillment in serving his masters to the utmost, and that meant interviews of sometimes agonizing length in order to understand exactly what they wanted.

The first wish had been wealth. You could usually make safe wager on that. Homam had taken care to unfold to Master that although a genie's power to grant wishes was near infinite by human understanding, it still was slave to certain rules. Master had found this fascinating, and, if the genie dared guess at Master's moods – pleasing. There was logic to the notion that a genie's feats did take energy, and energy needed to come from somewhere. The human race had a word in relatively wide parlance for that principle now: thermodynamics.

Homam had formerly relied on a long and hackneyed metaphor about the water in the oceans returning to the water in the sky returning to the water in the oceans. Thermodynamics was far more precise, even if it didn't provide the grandeur masters tended to expect. *Next time*, Homam noted to himself, *try saying it very slowly and loudly.*

Like many, Master had expressed concern that the energy might come from somewhere where it would do some living thing harm. The genie couldn't answer fully, since the complex interdependence of the stars and the galaxies would make any human's head pop long before you got anywhere worth describing, and their definition of life was hilariously narrow.

Instead, the genie just assured Master that the energy could be siphoned off a star with no planets around it far at the periphery of a galaxy with no life for thousands of light years, and that it could be summoned here essentially instantaneously via the higher dimensions that humans would never comprehend. And that if there was any chance of this appropriation of energy doing any measureable harm to any form of biology, it was far smaller than the chance of someone committing genocide by, say, muttering the word *Quackenbush* in the midst of the wrong alignment of gravitational influences.

Still, the genie had offered, since it required significantly less stolen star energy to, say, make Master extremely lucky at a game of chance, than it would be to summon great piles of gold bars out of nowhere (that business never got old to some masters), that this may please Master as the method to fulfill his first wish.

And it did please Master, who promptly won the State Lottery after Homam adjusted the air currents around some ping-pong balls and depressed the thought of certain numbers in the brains of a few people. A marvelously efficient execution of a very old wish, in terms of energy-to-wealth created and the near total lack of collateral misery and strife.

One of the consistent things about being a genie was that nearly all masters believed that wealth would free them of their anxieties and troubles, and thus allow them to discover the grander mission of their lives. The second wish usually had something to do with this, and this is the wish they were on now, as his Master sat on his $10,000 couch in his new living room in his new mansion.

Master had taken many notes before he had summoned the genie from the flask this time. This master wanted earnestly to get the assembly of these wishes right. He was not truly wise, but he was a little bit clever, and Homam knew that there was little more dangerous to the human race than people who were a little bit clever suddenly having a great deal of power.

"It sounds like a place you would spend a lot of time," he suggested to Master.

Master looked troubled at this, and consulted his notes. "Right! I forgot. Can we make it so time doesn't flow out here, in reality, while I'm in there? Like, if I went in there for an hour, I could come out and it would still be the same time I went in?"

"This is certainly possible, although Master risks shocking his friends and family by aging at a seemingly accelerated rate."

Master looked downright queasy now, and Homam was convinced that he had not thought of that beforehand, though he pretended otherwise. "Well, right, I mean, that goes without saying, right? I wouldn't get any older while I'm in there."

Homam was on familiar turf. He let himself bob down to eye level with Master in order to explain. "This is going to require some re-making of your brain, so that it can contain the memories of all your experiences in this place while not aging or decaying. I assume you want to remember them in detail, yes?"

Of course he assumed correctly. Master had some simple dreams for starters – to play at heroics, to mate effortlessly with women – things that he could probably do in real life were it not for his outsized trepidation about misery or embarrassment or imprisonment or death. He could no doubt fill a century in this fantasy space enacting just his ordinary, conscious hopes...and dream a few stars out of the universe as he did.

"How will it, I mean, the space, know? How will I talk to it?" Master betrayed his limits with his questions. Homam feigned ignorance, so Master could establish his thoughtfulness. "Will it be able to create exactly what I want – so there's no tricks or weird stuff?"

Homam could have said at this point that Master had more to fear from the weird desires in his own subconscious than any flaw in a wish Homam would build. But rather than engage with the furious denial that would no doubt follow, he simply promised that the means of summoning these fantasies would be entirely of Master's own making, and not just that, but that it would surprise him with its skill and intuition. "Like a supercomputer?" Master asked. The genie nodded, and, out of sheer petulance, elected not to supply any ethereal jangles to go with it.

At this point Master was just wrestling with amorphous paranoia. Even though a gaseous superbeing with a grandiose beard had already made him wealthy – and would make him wealthier still once some surprises Homam had buried somewhere called "the commodities market" blossomed – Master was still obviously greatly worried that such a treasure as they'd been discussing could be his at a word. It was a healthy attitude, from a certain perspective, although it had been known to try a genie's patience here and there.

Master made a nervous chuckle, and looked to be sweating through his new $300 shirt. "Well, um...is that it? Can you think of anything I'm leaving out?"

Homam had thought of many things that Master was leaving out. But being a genie did not bind him to full disclosure. Instead he gently suggested that the wished-for portal be made imperceptible to others, except those he could designate if he desired. This rather expanded the parameters of the wish, and led to a labored discussion of whether or not this wish could include the power to induce targeted amnesia in people should he decide that he no longer wanted to share his space outside space with them. Eventually it was settled that he could, in fact, choose people who could be brought in, and subsequently changed in similar ways so they could enjoy the non-aging, memory-retaining aspect of the experience, but that he would not be able to undo it. This would likely make him so cautious and mistrusting that he would never use the ability.

After more time and careful consultation of the notes he had scribbled with his new $1,000 pen, Master took a deep breath and declared himself ready to receive his wish. It was a substantial wish, the genie couldn't deny it, and both because of that and because this Master addressed him with respect, he gave it a really good show.

Waving his hands around, he created a swirling in the air, as if he was molding the fundamental flotsam of the universe so that it could be put into Master's service. He sapped some light from the room, and made Master's hairs stand on end – an old trick but a reliable one – and for a modern flourish he made a few light bulbs pop in their sockets. He left the $6,000 television intact.

There was an awesome rumble, and a shimmering sliver of starlight opened up over by the linen closet. A golden key floated out of this crack in the dimensions towards Master, with a sparkling thread dancing in the air behind it. It placed itself around Master's neck, and Homam knew that Master could figure out the rest. Satisfied that the theatrics had been appropriate, he brought his hands to rest, and let the Master's hairs fall once again to gravity.

Putting on a really wicked echo, he proclaimed, "Master, your wish is granted."

Master stared dumbly at the key, and at the little glow hovering in the air at hand height, waiting for that key's insertion. Homam would be going for a nap in the flask soon, but he did want to hang around for the next part.

Master still seemed to be seeking permission from some authority. "Can I? I mean – it's working and everything?"

Homam reluctantly admitted to himself that the echo probably needed to stay on for a bit longer: "It is complete – the space without space awaits you, and all your desires." He wondered if that last bit would embarrass Master, but it seemed to fly right by.

Master looked around his living room – checking to see if the porch door was locked and that sort of thing. He looked at his clothes, as if whoever or whatever was waiting in there might care what he was wearing. Just one of many old habits that wouldn't apply in a world that gave him everything he could want. And then, finally, he took the key from his neck, extended it towards that mesmerizing light...

And stopped to ask the genie, "What happens if I lose the key?"

Homam was nearly offended at the suggestion that he had not thought of that – or, worse, that it might be the linchpin of some cunning genie trick. He could certainly see a cohort of his pulling that one; making the key really light and slippery and uncooperative so that Master would only taste paradise once and then lose the key and scramble himself old and mad trying to find it again. But not Homam – Homam was better than that. "The key will always find you, Master."

Thus assured, Master slipped the key into the light, which then enveloped him, and he winked out of our dimension.

The next bit would be interesting. What Homam hadn't explained to Master was that time couldn't be completely frozen while he was outside of space. It could be slowed down significantly, sure, but if he spent a month in there then a good second or two would elapse in normal time. So Homam slowed his perceptions way down in order to get a good sense of just how long Master devoted to his first trip.

Although the language of the wish was new, like the first wish of wealth, this kind of second wish was hardly without precedent. The daunting thing about god-like power was always the bit about affecting – or possibly damaging or destroying – your fellow creatures. Guilt made people want loopholes, and who better to create them than genies?

But there was always a danger to this kind of wish, which is why Homam watched with excited curiosity. It took an awful lot of energy, this space outside of space. So much matter to create – and at the speed of dreaming, to boot. Most people, once they got accustomed to using this power, tended to use it relatively sparingly – something about the struggle of reality felt too necessary to abandon utterly.

There was that chance, though – that far, strange, chance – that this master would be one of the ones who simply forgot to leave. That, as years turned into centuries turned to ages in the realization of his little whims, so much matter would need to be created for the purpose that the whole of the Universe might be collapsed and pulled through that little pinhole in order to be available to his infinite service.

Life in its way would go on, and Master would never know that he was no longer outside time and space – it was better that way.

Homam waited, and wondered if this might be one of those times. It would mean a long nap, but third wishes after the destruction of the Universe tended to be really ripping.

❖

MY STORY OF THE MIDWAY

Water from the faucet; gargle and spit. My face in the mirror – older than it was yesterday. Sigh, hit the lights.

Into the bedroom. My wife is in a thick good book with her spectacles on. The kids are asleep. I have finished another day of my life. I slip under the blanket, hands under the pillow. Joints stretch and pop. I breathe, I breathe, I breathe.

Out goes the little lamp, and the shadows own the room. An alarm clock glows green and promises I will have another day tomorrow. It hasn't lied to me yet.

I don't know when, I never know when, but the moment comes and I am asleep.

⁕⁕⁕

The Devil walked into my dream announced by a massive noise: a roar and a fanfare mated. His skin was bronze and his jaw was proud. He arrived still and calm, with a mouth slyly arched to show that he knew I knew him.

"Who are you?" he asked softly, and in his confidence I was caught and held to answer. I gave him my name, and called myself a man, an American, raised Christian but not practicing, a storyteller, a husband, a father. His eyes grew; they were like the rippling, bottomless black fabric of the whole night sky. "I care about none of those things," he declared, "except that you are a storyteller."

When my dream began I had been in a simple room, with carpet and furniture and walls. It had all vanished beyond my notice.

"Are your stories true?" he asked. The words crawled under my skin, multiplied, collided and careened through my body, touching every part with a chill. I was standing my ground, or imprisoned to it; I couldn't tell the difference. I answered that while my stories were made up, I strived to base them on truth.

He laughed, and the rumble of it shook my heart. "You have it backwards," he assured me, and his laugh grew as he repeated himself. "You have it backwards."

He offered me a visit to Hell. He promised no fire or torment; none of the old things. He promised that I could leave when I chose only by asking him. "You are living and your soul is your own," he said. His confidence could swallow the Earth.

His only fee was that I tell the story of the going.

✶✧✶

In a moment I was in a field of abused grass: trampled, scrabbly and yellow, struggling out of the dirt for its brief, nasty time in the sun. It spread to every horizon, this holocaustic carpet, but with cunning mounds and slopes to suggest a path. The sky shone a harsh dirty-white, and I shrank under its light, feeling that something great must be watching me.

No air moved around me; this subtlety so strange as to make me stop. The hairs on my arms waited for the smallest tingle of a breeze, and the nothingness startled me. Was I breathing? Did it nourish me? Was I past nourishing?

I heard sounds behind a rise: creaks and rustles and chattering voices. The Devil's promise, so far, was true. There was no fire or torment. He knew my thoughts, and floated his voice into me from nowhere I could see.

"Do you want to leave? Or do you want to see?"

I felt cautious, an ancestral tingle carrying the memory of being prey. *It is only safe to leave,* I thought. *Why should I do anything else?*

I followed the sounds through the rive between rises, because I wanted to see.

＊⊙＊

A field of tents bit into the ground around the rise: a city of torn fabric and ropes. It was a carnival, an amusement with no signs or promises, just a mystery at every opening.

What were they wandering among the tents – imps or men withered and sapped? Short and ruddy, they moved leisurely, grunting and chattering in ways I couldn't understand. But they saw me, acknowledged me, and recommended some of the little pavilions around me with their gestures. Not to force, not to tantalize, simply to say – *this is what is done. Get on with it.*

The sky felt so bright and awesome that I had to want the dark.

I picked a tent at random and entered. The space yawned open before me and my eyes accepted the shadows and cheap filament bulbs strung to light the place. Imps lined the walls, bent for a good view. Silence settled like the snowfall.

A man stepped out before us from somewhere in the dark back. He wasn't changed or shrunken like the imps. He looked normal. So normal that I suddenly worried I couldn't see him at all: that my eyes might slide right around his white or tan or dark face and his lean or round or tall silhouette. I stopped knowing if he or she was a man at all. It was the most normal human I had ever seen: old and young, both or neither.

It stood so still. I waited for a move, a voice. But it only stood. And the imps around me were rapt. This unstrange sight, to them, was a font of fascination and delight.

I asked, "Who are you?" and was raucously shushed. Anyway, I received no answer.

The normal one turned around, walked two steps into the black, and the tent was empty.

∗◇∗

I followed a melody into the next tent. But the music wasn't the show. The music was the audience – heads keened up, they buzzed and hummed at the tent roof, and the sounds cascaded into weird clarity, like the living wave that ripples across the air made by birds at sunset.

Across from the audience, in an space strewn with sawdust, three robots stood before clothing racks. They were two tall and one small, making a family. The clothing racks held animal skins – a suit of alligator, of bear, of bull, a giant beetle, so many. The robots faced the crowd, hearing the song. From the notes they could glean a mood, changing moment to moment from yearning to apprehension to jangling ecstasy, and then the robot parents leaned back with decisive satisfaction, and moved to the racks to dress their robot boy.

They zipped him into a lizard, patient and still. They changed him into a silly little ostrich, then a deer, ready for a life of grace and terror. The changes went on and on, with no fatigue and no preference, following the tune.

When they dressed him as a spider I felt an enraged desire to crush him. I fought this only because of the horror of costing anyone a child. My foot lifted and I fought and felt the horror through and through.

And then with a change of key and a swift zip, the child was a pelican. A fish was in my hand, and I threw it.

"Are you a fisherman?" asked the Devil's voice.

I was man, an American, raised Christian but not practicing; a husband, a storyteller. Not a fisherman. A storyteller.

"Then stop catching fish," the Devil said, and I stepped from the tent. A robot child would never grow.

¦

The entrance of each tent was always too crowded, so I would exit from the other side. My memory of the path I had taken grew more slippery. It was a line in my mind that would vibrate and split and curl, flowering into more variations each time I reviewed it.

I had the Devil's promise, and that old apprehension that understood this was nothing to trust. But I could always ask; I could leave whenever I asked. I couldn't see any trick in this. So did I need to hold on to how I got here? Or did my obsession with it keep me from seeing what was in front of me?

I could see now that the imps looked less alike. I found distinctions in height and shape and hair, marks on their skin. Had I not paid attention before; had I been too concerned about the place and not the living things? Or had my eyes adjusted to that stark, decayed light?

A crowd of them had gathered around a rolling cart. It was serving morsels of something, and the crowd continued to grow, so much that the cart was soon gone from sight. I thought of a sweet sticky drop consumed by piling insects.

The crowd got their fill with extraordinary order – they passed food shoulder over shoulder to the back reaches. Then the whole hungry knot spread back into the carnival like a mound of sand slowly flattened by the vibrations of the earth. But the cart and its owner stayed behind with one more morsel in hand, and myself the only one who hadn't eaten.

I stepped forward and took it: wrapped in paper, an impeccable plain cake, heavy though small, speckled with sugar crystals that seemed to fracture the daylight. I didn't hesitate to bite, and soon it was gone and I felt satisfied. I turned over the paper, which was greaseless and crumbless. It had a fortune, written in tiny ink letters:

Be endless – for there is no such thing as a horizon.

I marched to the nearest edge of the carnival. Imps were mounting more tents, hoisting ropes and hammering pegs. And then I saw one apart from the rest. He walked with a weary step, dragging behind him a small plow. So he left no footprint, just this wedge in the dirt that stretched beyond my vision.

I fell in step beside him, and for a while we kept quiet company. He stopped to drink from a bottle strung around his neck, and it seemed the moment to ask. "What are you doing?"

He never turned his head. "I make a circle. I finish it, then I make a larger circle. I am on the third day of making this circle."

The Devil had promised no torments. "Why must you do this?" I probed. "What did you do?"

He resumed walking. "This is not punishment. I am in love with circles. You would do this too, if you loved them."

I stared at the line freshly turned behind him. It seemed absolutely straight to my eye. I felt a temptation to scuttle the dirt and break the line. Would it free him? Kill him? He called back without turning. "I cannot stop you from hurting my circles. I can only plead with you. Please do not hurt my circles – I love them."

"What if I want to cross one?" I called to him. If it were the choice of my freedom, I would hurt his love.

"Then sooner or later you would come upon another I love just as much."

At last I realized this was the first time I had understood the speech of any of them.

The Devil injected his question into my thoughts again. "Do you understand the story?"

I was a man, an American, raised Christian but not practicing, and I was a storyteller. So I riposted, "It's my job to tell, not to understand."

"Very good. Is it told?"

I looked at the mass of tents that surrounded me again. It grew faster than I could ever explore. To describe it all would be an eternal futility. Had I seen the Devil's trap?

"Why do you keep thinking I want to trap you? I just want a good story."

I knew it wasn't told. There had to be another way. A story was more than just the sum of descriptions. But I didn't know the path for this one yet. I needed to see more.

❋❋❋

I saw a thick, dusty coat, upright and moving by its own power, or maybe worn by someone invisible. The coat sat behind a desk, and just below an outstretched sleeve a quill pen seemed to pilot itself over a long, wide paper the color of flesh. The paper spilled off the sides of the desk, and was nearly filled with inked symbols. The pen paused after each symbol it made, and searched for a blank place to draw in.

I approached and I saw, hiding in the thicket of symbols, letters of the alphabet, but they were so few and small. All the others were foreign to me, and none were alike.

"Why is the alphabet here?" I asked.

With blinding speed, the quill lifted from the paper and flashed across it, tracing a pattern without touching. I recognized the alphabet letters lighting up in the order of the words I had spoken, along with some of the other shapes I didn't know.

The coat turned towards me and gestured extravagantly, as though speaking. Then its sleeve reached towards me, offering the quill. The quill floated up and bobbed in front of me, hopeful of something; what else could a pen want out of its existence but something on which to write? I rolled up a sleeve and offered the surface of my arm.

The quill nodded itself forward, accepting with courtesy, and then, with such delicate, tickling care, scripted me a message.

It is all the alphabet. It is the alphabet of every sound Man can make.

A strange optimism and amazement swelled in me. I thought of those few moments in my life when I had the sensation of seeing through the normal fabric of things to a flashed glimpse of the clockworks of the universe, where I was stunned to bewilderment by the possibilities.

I dared to ask: "Do we still make new sounds?" Again the quill stopped, lifted, and traced the question. Again the coat turned and danced its funny pantomime to respond. The quill returned to me, and I bared my other arm for its answer.

You do! However, I am running out of room, and it takes all my creativity to find new spaces for the sounds you make. I don't know what will force me to stop first. But it will end sometime.

I remembered that I had paper: the fortune from the food cart's cake, still folded in the pocket of my shirt. I pulled it out and looked at the fortune.

Be endless – for there is no such thing as a horizon.

I held it out, a dread sense of responsibility having overtaken all my wonder. "What if I gave you this?"

The fortune lifted from my hand, floated to the edge of the great paper, and seemed to join it, changing color and merging without a seam or stitch. The difference was so pitifully small.

The quill floated back, and chose a spot of flesh just below my chin, and traced a few final words there. I couldn't see them, and there was no mirror.

As I left the tent, the Devil's voice taunted me. "What powerful advice you had in your pocket. Why did you give it away?"

*※◇※

A human woman was wheeled into the tent on a plain gurney. Her body below the chest was covered by cloth, with gaps spaced along her torso and legs. An imp entered, walking with a meticulous slow step. He bore a small, silver tray with two flower buds resting in its center, beautifully unfurled. I swore their petals waved in beckoning even with no breeze.

The imp touched the edge of the tray against the crown of the woman's head. The flower buds lifted themselves and slowly flipped over onto her closed eyelids. The petals draped, and where you would have seen eyes were now the short clipped ends of the stems those buds wore when they were flowers. Glistening water cried down them.

This woman's body subtly collapsed into some deep rest. Her chest barely rose and fell.

The gurney was creaky-ratcheted down towards the floor. Seven more imps marched into the tent with the same formality, three each in lines along the gurney, and seventh in a spotless apron, who took the first imp's place behind the woman's head. His tray held the glistening fresh body of a fish; with perfect strokes he carved it into pink morsels.

These morsels he placed with perfect delicacy onto the woman's skin where it was exposed in the gaps of the cloth. The other imps waited in their places as he slid the morsels to the exact quarter-inch he desired. And then he kissed both of the sleeping woman's feet, bowed his head, and backed out of the tent.

The six imps that remained each raised a hand. Each pointed a single claw, and each sliced into the woman's skin, tracing around the fish pieces. They speared both fish and tissue with a claw from their other hand, lifted it to their mouths, and ate, chewing with delicate appreciation. Left behind was the red-raw new flesh, six square wounds paired and spaced along her length.

Revulsion swelled in me. But she hadn't woken, or even flinched. An imp saw my concern, and whispered in a scratchy tone, "She does not feel it. She volunteered for the experience."

I finished his sentence. "And that is why you worship her." I didn't know how that truth had found its way into me, but the imp acknowledged it with a bow.

"Do you understand why she would do this?" This was the Devil's voice again.

I had seen so much in my life. I was a man, an American, and a storyteller. "I feel it, but I don't understand it."

He replied, "How can a story claim a truth without an understanding?" It was a paradox deeper than a thousand receding mirror reflections, and it percussed so the very echo of it sounded like his deep, cruel laughter.

I wanted to defy the Devil, and to tell him that I no more owed him an explanation than I owed him my soul. But I believed if I pushed further into the carnival, I might find the key to his challenge, and at last tell the story so that it could be true and full, and even to make it understood.

I was done with this tent. The woman slept on.

❖❖❖

Imps seated in a clearing beckoned me over to them. They shifted where they sat, unstillable urgency teetering them like wind. I joined them at their encouragement and sat.

One by one, each imp lay a card in the dirt before them, playing a hand in some game. I saw no stakes, and didn't know the rules. But each placed their card, and when they were done they looked expectantly at me.

I looked down at my hand, which I thought to be empty. Yet there was a card there; somehow it had slipped into my grip and nestled, stiff and plastic. I turned it over to see its number and suit, but instead I saw an unresolving swirl, a snaking ink squiggle that would not rest into form.

I set it down and waited for the next action. But all the seated imps rose and scurried away, and others rushed into the clearing to replace them. Cards appeared in their hands and they played them in turns.

I tried to retrieve mine and play it again, but my fingers could not get under it even by digging. The card was played.

"But what are the rules? What have I bet? How many of us are playing?"

One imp played his card, then rose and walked right up to me. His head tilted dismissively downward, he pointed at me and grunted, "It says on your chest.

"It says: 'WE SHALL SEE.'"

And suddenly I ran, as far and fast from the game as I could.

Fabric flapped as I hustled among the tents, dodging and dancing wherever my heartbeat wanted. Mounting fear passed a threshold and became a trembling giddiness. I laughed, overpowered by it, heedless of path or my duty or any caution. I burst through a line of tents and once again was on the open plain.

And there were people there – humans like me, awake and standing with faces and voices and clothes and feelings.

It was a party, an unmistakably fine cocktail soiree. The people drank and laughed and drank and nodded and grinned so wide. They didn't behave as if there were no walls around them, or that the tents of the carnival were still spreading in their direction. They didn't even notice the dead grass under their beautiful shoes.

A determined crowd of imps scampered past my legs and into the midst of the people. They shinnied up the fancy guests like playground poles. One reached the top of a man, plunged his hands into the human's mouth, and spread it impossibly wide. Then he crawled right down the man's throat.

The man's throat bulged as the imp stuffed his way down, down into the stomach. Then the impossibly wide mouth rubber-snapped back to normal, and the conversation carried right on.

Over and over this happened, all over the beautiful crowd. And I realized I couldn't understand a word of what the people were saying.

✦✦✦

I tripped over a rope that snapped taut in my wandering path. It was thicker than any rope I had ever seen, thicker than my own leg. I heard dragging, and grunting, and a loud metallic screech.

I had become so accustomed to the sight of the imps erecting their tents that I had begun to filter the activity out of my considerations. It was the way that will disappears when we are sped up and zoomed out, and become specks tracing indistinguishable lines through brief lives. All the motions they made were the same, but now on a scale that called for thousands of them together.

I turned and saw the factory.

It was a massive structure, stone and metal, but it was billowing out of the ground and snapping into shape just like a fabric tent, raised by tugging of ropes, stretching, and pounding of spikes. Walls rose, then a chimney, then smoke from the chimney.

Massive doors took dimension. And the moment I saw them, I was inside it.

It was dark. I couldn't move. Sounds crashed down on all sides of me like storm waves – hisses and rusty scrapes, faraway screams, the sliding of chains. Heat and steam blasted my face. Sweat – I was sweating for the first time in my journey, and could feel the drops roll down my face.

There was light on one side, though I could see out of just one eye. I took in the vast gray space around me, desperate for detail. Why couldn't I move? My body felt cramped and bent, folded and stuffed into a box and nothing was where it belonged. My leg might have been up by my head, my arms both stuck under me on the same side.

A machine roared. My body bumped and started to slide. I was rolling on an old conveyer belt, carried somewhere I couldn't see. Panic rose in me, my vision shook and blurred and I couldn't move. The metal machines slammed and clattered louder and closer and I couldn't move. Voices howled out, screaming out names I didn't know or remember, and I couldn't move.

"You're in no danger," the Devil promised.

"I don't believe you," I answered in my mind.

"I haven't lied to you at all. You are alive. You are only dreaming."

One female voice cut through, one I swore I knew, and it screamed, over and over. "You're killing him! You're killing him!" I heard crying in the words, but I didn't know who she was. All I knew was that I was rolling to the machine. The hissing, ravening yawn it made was for me.

I was a man; I was a storyteller. I had made a deal with the Devil that he would show me Hell if I would tell the story. He wanted to hear the story, he wanted to hear a good story. Was the story finished? Was it true? Did I understand it? I had taken those questions as my own. My body was frozen and all I could think was, *Is the story told? Is the story told?* The noise, the noise, the fear and the noise. *Is the story told?*

"I want to leave."

"You want to go back?"

"Yes, yes, I want to go back!"

"Is this really the whole story?"

"I don't know, I just want to go!"

"You said you wanted to tell me a good story; the whole story."

"It's done. The story is done when I can no longer tell it."

"Really?" His voice swelled with raging cruelty. "Who are you to claim something like that?"

I was a storyteller...I was a storyteller...

What was my name?

What was my name?

"I have told the story I want to tell and I want to leave now."

And everything was black and silent and I hovered in it.

❊❊❊

"Do you see how I kept my word?" the Devil said. He did not appear.

The familiar vibrated around me; I was in the dreamworld of my own mind.

"You see what you have done," he said.

"Yes," I answered. I understood. And it made me feel safe and human and alive. But not strong. Just small.

"I will leave you with a final question," said the Devil. "Remember what you saw. Write about it. But also ask: did you ever really see Hell? Or was all of this just the road I offered, and you quit before you got there?"

And with the instant disinterest of a child dropping a toy, he released me.

I could breathe again, and in those slippery seconds that dribble our night visions away I turned back into all the things my life had made me. But I didn't know the answer to his question.

✳✳✳

I am awake. I am alive. There is my wife. There is my alarm clock. The day wants things from me. My family is important. My work is important. The newspaper assures me that everything it has to tell me is so important.

What did I dream about?

✳✳✳

How did you sleep?

ABOUT THE AUTHOR

Nicholas Thurkettle is a writer of screenplays, stage plays, and books, and an actor on stage, camera, and audio-wave. Born in Los Gatos, California, he grew up in the suburbs of Cincinnati, Ohio, turned teenage in Huntington Beach, California, and studied at Bradley University in Peoria, Illinois, where he earned B.A. degrees in Theatre Performance and Music. He has worked, among many other jobs, as a feature film story executive, a limousine driver, a film critic, a luggage salesman, a teacher of screenwriting, a professional smeller for a Sanitation Department, and something called a "data migration project supervisor." His first novel, *Seeing by Moonlight* (co-written with MF Thomas), debuted on all digital platforms in Autumn 2013 and was called "an intriguingly dark thriller, with enough twists and turns to keep the reader turning pages up until the rather surprising conclusion" by IndieReader. A second collaboration with MF Thomas, *A Sickness in Time*, is expected to be released by the end of 2015. He produced, wrote, and directed the short film *Samantha Gets Back Out There*, expected to play film festivals in 2016. He is a proud member of the Writers Guild of America and the Orange County Playwrights Alliance, an Artistic Associate with Shakespeare Orange County, and a producer/writer/performer with the award-winning audio drama podcast *Earbud Theater*. He currently lives in Southern California.

CONNECT

http://www.nicholasthurkettle.com
https://www.twitter.com/NThurkettle
https://www.facebook.com/NThurkettle

❖

Thank you for purchasing and reading Stages of Sleep. I hope you will take the time to leave a rating and review wherever you purchased it; it makes such a difference for independent creators. And I hope we meet again. My work takes me to a lot of places – do join me in some of the others. –NT

-END-